THE FLYING SAUCER
MYSTERY

NANCY DREW MYSTERY STORIES®

THE FLYING SAUCER MYSTERY

by

Carolyn Keene

Illustrated by
Ruth Sanderson

WANDERER BOOKS

Published by Simon & Schuster, New York

Copyright © 1980 by Stratemeyer Syndicate
All rights reserved
including the right of reproduction
in whole or in part in any form
Published by Wanderer Books
A Simon & Schuster Division of
Gulf & Western Corporation
Simon & Schuster Building
1230 Avenue of the Americas
New York, New York 10020

Manufactured in the United States of America
10   9   8   7   6   5   4   3

WANDERER and colophon are trademarks of Simon & Schuster

NANCY DREW and NANCY DREW MYSTERY STORIES are
trademarks of Stratemeyer Syndicate, registered in the United States
Patent and Trademark Office

Library of Congress Cataloging in Publication Data

Keene, Carolyn, pseud.
The flying saucer mystery.

(Her Nancy Drew mystery stories; 58)
SUMMARY: Nancy and friends, in search of information about a
UFO, become involved in another mystery involving the
inheritance of an old man who lives in the forest.
[1.   Mystery and detective stories] I.   Sanderson,
Ruth. II.   Title.
PZ7.K23Nan no. 58   [Fic]   79-24954

ISBN   0-671-95514-4
ISBN   0-671-95601-9   pbk.

Contents

1

A Spooked Horse

"Good-bye! Good luck! And be careful, Nancy. This new mystery you want to solve sounds dangerous!"

The words of farewell were spoken by Mrs. Hannah Gruen, the Drews' housekeeper. She kissed the eighteen-year-old, titian-blond girl and hugged her affectionately.

"I'll be *very* careful," Nancy promised, adding lightly, "Has anyone got the best of your favorite detective yet?"

"No, but there's always a first time!" Hannah replied as Nancy jumped into her father's car.

Without further discussion, Carson Drew, a distinguished lawyer, headed for the River Heights airport. As they pulled up to the terminal, two girls stepped out of a sedan.

"Bess and George!" Nancy exclaimed.

Bess Marvin and George Fayne were cousins and were Nancy's closest friends. The three girls, who were going on a camping trip in the Shawniegunk Forest, now set their large backpacks and sleeping bags on the sidewalk in front of the terminal entrance. Mr. Drew and Mrs. Fayne said they would park their cars and come back to see the girls off.

"I had to leave so much at home!" complained Bess. She was Nancy's age and pretty—but slightly plump.

"Well, I brought lots of rain gear and not much else." George giggled. She was an attractive slim brunette. "If it doesn't rain, I'll be out of luck!"

"If it does"—Bess frowned—"I'll be wetter than a guppy."

"You mean a whale!" George laughed.

"Thanks a lot, George!" her cousin replied, narrowing her eyes.

That was Nancy's signal to lead the way to the ticket counter where the girls' camping equipment was weighed and checked in. They each picked up a ticket and seat assignment, and walked to the departure gate.

Mrs. Fayne and Mr. Drew arrived just a few minutes before takeoff. As the boarding announcement was made, Mr. Drew kissed Nancy. "I hope you solve the mystery, honey," he said as a twinkle came into his eyes. "But be on the lookout for strange creatures in the forest!"

Bess shuddered. "What do you mean, Mr. Drew?"

Nancy's father refused to explain further. "You'd better hurry, or you'll miss your plane."

The girls scooted quickly through the check-in area and soon were seated side by side in the plane.

"I had no idea this trip would be dangerous," Bess said. "I thought it was going to be fun."

"It should be," Nancy replied. "After all, I did promise you a mystery, and isn't solving mysteries fun? I'll tell you more about this one when we join the boys."

The trip had been arranged by Mr. Drew. At his suggestion, the girls had asked their boyfriends to meet them in a little town at the foot of the wooded Shawniegunk Mountain where the small plane would land. Jan and Hal Drake, their guides, were to be there also.

During the two-hour flight, the three teenagers hardly spoke to one another. Each was wondering what lay ahead. Bess and George knew there was bound to be danger—as well as a thrilling adventure—on a trip with Nancy.

By the time the plane landed, the boys were already there. Tall, athletic Ned Nickerson was

3

Nancy's boyfriend. Burt Eddleton, a short, husky blond, was George's friend, and Bess's special companion was blond, green-eyed Dave Evans.

The boys introduced the Drakes, an attractive couple who had lived in the area since their marriage a few years before.

"I'm sure all of you are going to have as much fun here as we do," said Jan, a vivacious blond with streaks of gray in her hair. "We love to camp out and ride through this magnificent forest."

"Sounds wonderful," Nancy replied. "Is everything set for go?"

Hal smiled. "At your service. Follow me."

The young people picked up their backpacks and sleeping bags and followed Jan and Hal to a long shed where several horses were tied up.

"Here's your means of transportation," said Hal. He was a tall, slender man with a ruddy complexion and a firm jaw. His mouth turned up at the corners in an engaging grin.

"Oh, how marvelous!" George exclaimed, dropping her things in a heap and admiring the line of horses. She patted and spoke to each one while Hal and the others conferred over which animals they ought to use.

"What's the name of my horse?" Nancy asked, as she mounted easily.

"Susan B," Hal told her as she leaned forward to hug the beautiful, young bay mare.

"You and I are going to solve a big mystery!" she whispered to Susan B.

Ned mounted his horse and rode alongside Nancy, saying, "This is Goalpost. Appropriate?"

"Appropriate, but I don't believe it." Nancy smiled. "Somebody must've known the captain of Emerson College's football team was coming. Even so, I'm sure you're not going to find any goalposts in the forest."

"But I can run for a touchdown!" Ned quipped. "The solution to the mystery may be right there."

Within minutes the string of riders and horses started off. It was not long before they came to the forest and followed Jan up a steep trail.

They had ridden about an hour when the stony path led them to a pleasant spot by a mountain brook.

"Oh, doesn't it smell wonderful here?" Bess said, breathing in the pine scent. "And look at all the wild flowers."

Sweet-smelling woodbine was entwined around stately trees and white flowers peeked through ground shrubbery.

Jan signaled for the procession to halt. The riders dismounted, allowing the horses to rest while Jan unloaded a sack of picnic food from one of the two packhorses.

Before letting the horses graze, Hal and the boys led them to the brook for a refreshing drink. After tethering two of the horses, everyone sat down on the ground to enjoy a variety of sandwiches, as well as tomato juice and nutcake.

"Now, Nancy, let's hear about the mystery we're going to solve," Ned suggested, after tasting a ham sandwich.

Nancy leaned forward and spoke softly. "Dad received word—secretly of course—that several people in the vicinity of Shawniegunk Mountain had seen a UFO come down and disappear. Some of them even hunted for it."

"Was it from outer space?" Bess quivered.

"Everyone thought so," Nancy said, causing her friend's look of alarm to change to fright.

"Didn't they notify the authorities?" Burt asked.

Nancy shook her head. "Apparently not. They were afraid of being laughed at. Anyway, they failed to find the UFO. Nevertheless, they were sure it had landed. There was a similar rumor about ten years ago, but nothing came of it."

"And we're supposed to find this flying saucer?" George inquired.

"Yes, we are," Nancy replied. "Not only find it but try to learn something about the craft and where it came from."

Dave grunted. "That sounds like a big order."

"But a real challenge," Ned added.

The words were scarcely out of his mouth when

Bess screamed loudly and jumped to her feet.

"What's the matter?" George asked her cousin.

Too frightened to answer, Bess merely pointed. A snake was wriggling away from her!

Hal ran to see if the snake was poisonous. He called back, "It won't hurt us."

Bess was still shaking. "It cr-crawled r-right across my b-boot!" she stammered. "I thought snakes didn't like people. I thought they stayed away from them!"

"That's usually true," Hal agreed. "But even snakes have an appetite for good home cooking."

"So you scared off your soul mate!" George teased.

Ignoring the remark, Bess declared that from now on she was going to eat standing up. "And I plan to walk around a lot, too."

Her friends laughed.

As Bess spoke, her eyes fastened on the slithering reptile. It was crawling toward the horses.

"The snake's going for my horse!" George gasped. "I must stop it!"

Before she could, however, the snake paused in back of the animal, then slowly wriggled up her rear leg. Instantly it spooked the horse, causing him to throw off the snake and run off at breakneck speed into the dense forest.

"Oh!" George exclaimed. "Burt, come quickly!"

7

Together they raced after the galloping horse but could not catch it. Meanwhile, the rest of the riders were trying to calm the other agitated animals and keep them from bolting, too. Ned and Dave offered to take their horses and go after the runaway.

Nancy clung to her horse's bridle and talked gently to the mare. She was having trouble with Susan B, who appeared to be terrified. Finally the horse settled down.

Burt was shamefaced. "It was so stupid of me not to tie the runaway horse when she finished drinking in the stream."

"She's so gentle and obedient," George remarked quietly, almost unaware of Burt's arm around her shoulder. "I hope she comes back."

Jan and Hal tried to comfort the distraught girl, too. "Horses hate snakes," Hal said, "and with a scare like that, yours would have pulled free anyway."

"What would you do if a snake crawled up your leg?" Jan added.

This made George and the others smile. "I think we'd all run!" she said.

While the campers waited for the two boys to return, they packed up, ready to move on. In twenty minutes Ned and Dave reappeared, leading George's mount. Excitedly, the girl ran to her horse and got astride.

Once more the group was on the move. Jan led them higher and higher up the mountain.

At one point Bess remarked, "I'll bet the view from here would be gorgeous if we could see through the trees."

Jan agreed and said that before dark they would reach an area where they could see for miles. "Hal and I think someone camped at the spot for quite some time, even cleared a little section of the forest and grew a vegetable garden. In any case, it will be a good place for us to camp."

When the riders arrived at their destination, Jan suggested, "Why doesn't everyone unpack for the night? I'll start cooking supper."

"May I help?" Bess asked eagerly.

"If you like," Jan said, removing a sack from one of the packhorses.

A few minutes later she cried out, "Oh, we left our cooking utensils at the picnic spot! How could I have been so forgetful and left one of the sacks on the ground?"

Nancy offered to go back.

"Not alone," Jan answered quickly. "I'll tell you what: we'll draw lots. I'll get four sticks and mark one, then we'll choose by couples. Whoever gets the marked stick will go."

Nancy was delighted when she and Ned drew the lucky stick. Instantly she mounted Susan B and Ned mounted Goalpost, and they set off down the narrow trail. The trip, Jan and Hal figured, would take at least an hour.

When two hours had gone by and it was dark, the riders still had not returned. Everyone was worried.

"Nancy and Ned are good horsemen," Bess said, "but lots of things could have happened."

A little while later Jan lay down and put her ear to the ground. "I hear horses coming," she called out.

As she stood up, the campers were startled by eerie screams in the distance.

2

The Wildcat

The campers froze with fear when they heard the screams in the quiet forest.

Bess cried out frantically, "Nancy and Ned must have been attacked by a wild animal! Oh, what'll we do?"

"We must find them!" George shouted.

"I'm sure," said Hal, "those screams were coming from the north."

"I'd say just the opposite," George countered. "What do you think, Burt?"

"West," he answered, "and Dave thinks east."

Everyone felt helpless. Finally Jan spoke up. "I believe those screams were from a wildcat. I've heard similar ones before."

Bess was even more terrified. "Oh, Nancy and Ned may have been clawed to pieces!" she exclaimed.

George looked severely at her cousin. "Don't say such things!" she flashed back. "Let's hope Nancy and Ned are nowhere near a wildcat."

As a matter of fact the couple was not far from the menacing cat. They had found the missing bag of kitchen utensils, fastened it to Ned's saddle, and started back to camp. Unfortunately, they had taken the wrong branch of a trail which led them away from their destination. Unaware of their mistake at first, they kept riding. Finally, however, the sun set and as darkness came on, the two riders stopped and looked at each other.

"Are you thinking the same thing I am?" Nancy asked. "We're lost!"

"I'm afraid you're right," Ned conceded. "We'd better turn around and head for the other trail."

Susan B and Goalpost started off in the opposite direction. A few feet before they reached the fork, Nancy caught sight of two glowing eyes and the shadowy outline of an animal on a branch of a pine tree.

"Ned!" she called. "Look up there! Some creature is watching us!"

As the boy gazed upward, the animal hissed, then broke the stillness with an unearthly scream. Chills

13

went up and down the riders' spines. The frightened horses reared and whinnied.

"We'd better run for it," Ned suggested, urging Goalpost to go fast. "It's a wildcat!"

The gleaming eyes in the tree fascinated Nancy. As she rode past the cat, she wondered if the beast would spring at her and Susan B. Nancy's heart pounded.

Suddenly she and Ned were startled by the sound of a sharp whistle followed by the soothing voice of a man.

"Now, Kitty, behave yourself!" he said coaxingly. "Stop trying to scare folks!"

At once the glowing eyes sank back. Evidently the animal had jumped out of the tree and disappeared into the dark forest.

"Who's there?" Ned called, as he and Nancy stopped.

"Old Joe," came the reply.

A light was shone in the riders' direction. A couple of minutes later a tall, slender man of about seventy appeared. His hair was gray and he had a beard that was as unkempt as his clothes. Was he one of the "strange creatures" her father had warned her about? Nancy wondered.

The man's friendly smile, however, and his kindly blue eyes made her dismiss the idea.

"Howdy!" he greeted the couple. "What are you

folks doing riding around in the dark? You're strangers here, aren't you?"

Quickly Nancy explained, then introduced herself and Ned. "We're camping with a group of friends a little way up the trail."

Ned added, "You called yourself Old Joe. Will you tell us what your full name is? And do you live around here?"

"My full name is Joseph Austin. Folks in the village gave me the nickname of Old Joe. I kind of liked it, so I kept it. I rarely use my last name."

"By the way, many thanks for scaring off that hissing creature," Nancy said. "What was it? A wildcat?"

"Yes."

"We were sure he was going to attack us."

"Oh, Kitty, as I call her, wouldn't attack unless something bothered her."

"Well, she sure wasn't friendly to us," Nancy grumbled.

Old Joe laughed. "Oh, it had nothing to do with you directly. I have a dog, Trixie. She was teasing Kitty. I suspected that, and came up here to see what was going on. Then I heard Kitty scream, and hurried. I must say it was a surprise to meet you folks."

"You mentioned a dog," Ned said.

"Oh, Trixie is too smart to let Kitty get the jump on

her," Old Joe replied. "She likes to tease Kitty but when the wildcat gets enough of it, she hisses and spits at the dog, even screams sometimes. Kitty and I have known each other for a long time. In fact she was just a kitten when we first became acquainted. Her mother must have abandoned her and she kind of brought herself up. I leave food out for her up near my cabin. It's some distance from here. You must come and visit me there."

Old Joe explained that he was a naturalist by preference. "I was in business once in the city but I didn't like it. As soon as I made enough money to retire I came up here where I used to spend my summers as a boy.

"Now all I do is study the behavior of wild animals toward man. Most won't attack unless they're extremely hungry, or are protecting their young, or are frightened or threatened by a human being or another animal.

"Of course, this doesn't apply to tigers," the naturalist added. "They'll attack for no reason at all."

Nancy remarked, "Wildcats and tigers are related, though, aren't they?"

"They're distant cousins. I'm glad there aren't any tigers in the United States. You know," he went on, "so far as is known, man is not the natural source of food supply for any other creature. I believe that man's worst enemy is man himself."

Nancy and Ned liked the elderly gentleman more

and more. He was not only a naturalist but a philosopher as well.

"We're heading for our camp," Nancy said. "Wouldn't you like to ride along and meet our friends?"

Old Joe chuckled. "I'd like that very much, but to tell you the truth, I prefer walking."

He and the riders followed the trail which Nancy and Ned had missed, and shortly they arrived at the camp.

"Oh, thank goodness, you're all right!" Bess said, hugging Nancy.

Everyone was overjoyed to see that she and Ned and the horses were safe. They also were delighted to meet Old Joe, who captured their hearts immediately with his quiet sense of humor and evident love of nature.

The campers had built a fire and now they all sat around it, listening to the comforting crackle, while supper was served to the latecomers.

"I don't buy much food from the store," Old Joe said. "I get practically everything I eat from in the woods."

Bess's eyes opened wide. "You mean you might eat wildcat meat?"

The man's eyes twinkled. "No, but I do catch rabbits and groundhogs. One of the best dishes you'd ever want to eat is groundhog stew."

That did not sound appealing to Bess, but she kept

silent. Old Joe said there was good fishing in the mountain streams and all sorts of delicious berries and plants.

"One of my favorite dishes is stewed wild rose leaves."

Although Bess knew she was being teased, the plumpish girl decided that if she ate some of this natural food, the scale might reflect the benefits. She was always making promises to herself to modify her eating habits, but never actually followed through.

The rest of the campers were more interested in hearing about Old Joe's adventures in the forest. He entertained them with wildlife stories including one about his rescue of a bear cub.

"Got himself caught in somebody's makeshift trap. I set him free but you know what? He followed me home! Craziest bear I ever met. Well, I figured he was hungry so I fed him and told him to scat. But next morning he was scratching at the door just like a puppy."

"Does he still live with you?" Bess asked in amazement.

"Oh, no. He only stayed with me until he was old enough to go out into the forest and forage for himself. Never did see that bear again, so I imagine he survived on his own."

Now the elderly man stood up and said he must

18

get back to his cabin. "I expect all of you to come over and visit me. My little cabin and everything in it is handmade," he remarked. "I'm rather proud of my accomplishments and I'd like you to see them. You've shared your food with me, so now it's my turn to feed you."

The campers thanked Old Joe for the invitation, then said good night. Suddenly George stopped him and asked, "Have you ever seen a flying saucer around here?"

The campers waited breathlessly for an answer.

3

Mountain Mishap

Old Joe looked at the group, startled. "You've heard about the flying saucer?" he asked in surprise. "I thought only a few natives knew about that."

Nancy told the naturalist that a client of her father's had contacted him and divulged the secret. "Dad is a lawyer. He said people around here who knew about the flying saucer were afraid to report it for fear of being laughed at."

Old Joe smiled. "I think that's partially true. As for myself, I never could be sure whether it was a real unidentified flying object from outer space or some government experimental aircraft."

"Then you've seen it?" Ned asked.

The naturalist said indeed he had. "The saucer usually appears at night and has very bright lights. I've seen only white lights, but some folks say at times they're red, other times green, and even yellow.

"One man reported seeing the whole saucer turn bright red. It looked as if it were ready to burn up, but the thing flew away and disappeared."

Old Joe's listeners were intrigued by the strange story. All of them hoped that the mysterious flying saucer would return soon so they, too, might see it.

Dave asked, "Do the people who have seen it think there are human beings aboard?"

The naturalist smiled and shrugged. "Nobody's ever seen anyone come out. But I'd say one thing. If humans are aboard, they must be the best pilots in the whole universe."

Burt added with a chuckle, "And they're flying a super craft."

Old Joe said he really had to leave. Again he invited the group to come to his log cabin. "I'll show you some crude drawings I made of the flying saucer."

"That's great!" George remarked. "It's too bad you didn't take any photographs of it."

The naturalist said that some of the local people had tried to, but their high-speed cameras had been unable to capture anything but a blur.

"That's strange," Nancy remarked under her breath.

"I'll give you directions to my place," Old Joe said. He asked for paper and pencil, and drew a map of trails to his cabin. When he finished the zigzagging line, he looked squarely at Nancy. "I have a mystery of my own that I'd like you to solve," he said. "I'll tell you about it when you come to see me."

Intrigued by the prospect of another mystery, Nancy wondered what it might be, but Old Joe gave no hints. The campers decided they would call on him the next morning, and the naturalist was delighted.

After he had gone, Nancy thought excitedly, maybe Old Joe's mystery concerns his cabin. He did make a point of telling us that everything in it is handmade.

The following morning the campers packed up their belongings. Jan made sure this time that nothing was left behind.

"All set!" she called at last.

Everyone mounted a horse. Hal rode in front, carrying Old Joe's map. It led them onto a narrow side trail which apparently was a dry brook that became a torrent of water when there were cloudbursts or melting snow. Now the path was filled with small stones.

The riders had not gone far when Ned, who was following Nancy, suddenly cried out, "Goalpost has gone lame!"

At once, Nancy reined in Susan B and dismounted quickly to examine Goalpost's hooves.

"There's a stone wedged in this one," Nancy said, as she carefully lifted Goalpost's right foreleg.

She hurried back to her horse, opened the saddlebag, and took out a hoof pick. With Ned's assistance, she managed to dislodge the stone.

She patted the horse's nose and gave him a little hug, saying, "Now do you feel better, you nice old thing?"

Ned smiled. "Thanks for your help, Nancy." He, too, patted the animal.

By this time their friends were out of sight. When Nancy and Ned caught up with them, the group had stopped to discuss what they should do next.

"The forest is becoming more and more impenetrable," Hal announced. "It's impossible for the packhorses to get through because the trees are so close together. I suggest we tie them here and go on to Old Joe's without them. I'll check our walkie-talkies in case we get split up."

He examined the compact radiotelephones that were being carried in his and Jan's saddlebags. "They're okay," Hal said a few minutes later. "Let's go on. If any place is too narrow to pass through, pull your legs, saddlebags, and stirrups to the back of your horse."

Bess called out from the rear of the line, "Where are we going? I don't see the trail anymore."

"That's true," Hal replied somberly. "From here on it seems to be just a series of deer tracks. Let's hope they'll lead us right to Old Joe's cabin."

Ten minutes later George, who was riding directly behind Hal, pointed ahead. "Now what do we do?" she inquired.

As the others drew near, they could see an enormous fallen tree trunk blocking their path. Its diameter was higher than the backs of their horses.

"What a monster!" Dave exclaimed. "I wonder how tall the tree was."

The group dismounted, tied the horses, and spread out along the giant trunk.

Ned remarked, "My guess is that this oak must be over fifty feet long."

Bess stood back to admire it, saying, "What a gorgeous tree it must have been when it stood. How old do you think it is?"

"Anybody know how to read tree rings?" Ned asked.

Jan made her way to the end of the trunk where it had broken off. Unfortunately the tree had splintered apart and the rings could not be read accurately.

"Sorry," she said. "Probably Old Joe can tell us because it looks as though the tree trunk has been lying here a long time."

"One thing is certain," Hal added. "It wasn't sawed down. The tree fell either because it was diseased or because it was struck by lightning."

Burt had walked to the other end of the tree and announced that it would be impossible to get through the limbs and branches without a lot of hacking.

"We must have taken a wrong turn," the boy said. "If Jan's right, then I doubt Old Joe would have sent us this way."

Jan consulted the hand-drawn map. "Let's climb over and go the rest of the way on foot," she suggested.

"Yes, let's," Bess agreed. "We've been riding for hours and I'm starved. I bet Old Joe will have a good lunch for us."

Her cousin George teased, "I hope you'll like the menu. Remember, he lives on goodies from the forest. You'll probably have a broiled bullfrog, tasty worm salad, and for dessert, persimmons to pucker your tongue."

Everyone except Bess laughed. She made a face. Now the campers scrambled up the trunk and sat astride it the best they could.

To their dismay the group discovered they were

at the precarious edge of a steep decline at the foot of which there was a rushing stream filled with rocks, some of them large and treacherous.

Jan asked, "What do you say, everybody? Do we go ahead or turn back?"

For several uneasy seconds no one answered. Then Nancy said, "I think we should try it. Old Joe is expecting us and remember, he wants to tell us about his personal mystery. I'm dying to learn what it is so I can try to solve it. Besides, I want to see his sketches of the UFO; don't you?"

Ned concurred. "Isn't that the purpose of this trip?"

The others agreed. Jan suggested they go in pairs. "Take it slow and easy on the descent. Remember the saying, 'Haste makes waste,'" she cautioned. "Let's hope we can walk along the stream, which I think is the one on Old Joe's map."

Ned jumped down first and caught Nancy's hand as her feet touched the ground. The Drakes went next, followed by George and Burt. None of them had mishaps.

"Our turn," Dave told Bess. "There's nothing to worry about. I'll go first and catch you. Okay, partner?" Before he jumped, Dave paused for an answer.

Suddenly Bess said, "Wait! I—I'm so dizzy."

Instantly she lost her balance and rolled off the

trunk down the mountainside. There were fewer trees and bushes on the slope, evidently because of logging operations. Bess began to tumble faster.

"Oh, no!" Dave cried out, jumping off the trunk.

He dashed after her and caught his foot in a trailing vine that almost caused him to plunge headfirst. By now, Bess was far ahead of him and rolling rapidly toward the turbulent rock-filled water!

4

Trixie, Lifesaver

Quickly Dave regained his balance. He dug both heels into the mountainside as he ran to rescue Bess. She was only a few feet away from the dangerous stream!

Too far away to assist the helpless girl, the other campers watched in horror. Would Dave reach Bess before she fell among the jagged rocks and injured herself badly? She might even drown!

Without any warning, a large retriever bounded from among the trees. With lightning-fast leaps, the dog got to Bess. She grabbed the girl's belt in her teeth, braced herself against the hillside, and stopped Bess's descent in the nick of time.

"Oh, thank goodness!" George murmured.

Within seconds Dave was bending over the girl. She was unconscious and badly scratched.

"Bess! Bess!" he cried out, patting her cool, clammy cheeks.

The dog now stood alongside her, whining and looking at Dave for orders.

By then, Nancy, Ned, and the other campers had hurried back along the stream. Jan, who said she was a nurse, examined the unconscious girl for broken bones and concluded there were none.

Meanwhile, Nancy and George took wads of tissues from their backpacks, dipped them in the cold water, and applied them to Bess's forehead and the back of her neck. Ned and Burt daubed more cold water on her scratched face and arms. Presently Bess opened her eyes but said nothing.

Nancy whispered to her, "I'm so glad you aren't badly hurt, Bess. Why don't you lie right here until you feel better?"

For nearly ten minutes, Bess rested, then opened her eyes again. Finally, with Dave's help, she sat up.

"I don't think I'd better walk any farther. You all go along without me," she said quietly. Just then she noticed the retriever. "Where did you come from?" she asked the dog, who was wagging her tail.

"She saved your life," Dave told Bess, and explained what the animal had done. "I don't know where she came from."

Bess hugged the beautiful dog and thanked her. In reply, the lovely animal leaped out of her grasp, then ran back and forth along the stream, barking.

"Why is she doing that?" Bess asked.

Nancy guessed that the retriever wanted them to follow her. "Are you Trixie? Are you Old Joe's dog?" the girl detective asked.

The animal wagged her tail briskly and gave a number of short barks.

Nancy laughed. "I think this is Trixie and she wants to take us to her master's cabin." She patted the animal. "Okay, Trixie. Wait until we get the horses and then you lead us to Old Joe."

Jan said she would stay with Bess until the others returned. "I suggest that you leave one of the walkie-talkies with us so we can communicate with you if necessary."

Burt reminded, "It's going to be tough getting the horses down here. They can't climb over that tree trunk. We'll have to bypass it somehow."

"Right," Dave agreed. "We don't want any broken legs."

It took some doing to bring the horses down the mountainside. When they all arrived, one of the walkie-talkies was unpacked and left with Bess and Jan.

The other campers mounted and followed Trixie.

She stayed close to the bank of the stream. The going was rough but uneventful.

As a crudely built log cabin came into view, Trixie hurried on alone, barking wildly. Old Joe came outside immediately and welcomed the group with a big smile.

After counting the number of visitors, he asked, "Where are the other two?"

Nancy explained and added that Trixie was indeed a heroine.

The naturalist praised his pet. "I sent her to find you folks," he said. "I was afraid you might get lost. Evidently she met you at the right moment."

He invited the group to tie up their horses and come into the cabin. As he had told them, it was very unusual. It consisted of a single room with everything he needed in it.

In one corner stood a hand-carved wooden bed. The coverlet had been made from wild goat hide. Several bearskin rugs lay on the floor. The walls were covered with deer heads, and stuffed chipmunks and mounted birds adorned the windows. There was a huge stone fireplace next to which stacks of wood were piled high.

A large wooden dresser stood along one wall of the room. On top was a small wooden barrel holding a beautiful bouquet of wild flowers.

"This is lovely," Nancy remarked, leaning over to smell them.

Old Joe opened the top drawer to display the wooden forks, knives, and spoons he had made. Some of them were short and others very long. The latter, he explained, were used for holding meat over an open fire.

Were the blunt-looking knives sharp enough to cut meat? the onlookers wondered. The naturalist read their thoughts and suggested that the boys try them out. Ned picked up one and examined the edge. He almost cut his finger!

"It's sharp all right," he commented.

Old Joe laughed, then said, "I guess we'd better get some lunch ready." He called to Trixie. "Go fetch us some fish from the stream," he ordered, explaining to his guests, "She is an expert at catching trout in her teeth. When she brings them up here, how about you boys preparing them for cooking? Do you have hunting knives with you?"

"Yes," they chorused.

"Good. Then you girls can set up a three-legged spit to hang the fish on," Old Joe suggested, "while the boys gather some dry wood from the forest to make the outdoor fire for cooking it."

"All right," Nancy said, "but first I want to check on Bess."

She soon made contact with her walkie-talkie. Bess said she was better. "But I got really scared when we saw a giant staring at us from among some trees."

"A what?" Nancy asked in disbelief.

"A giant. He's a real tall Indian with his hair pulled over half his face. He had on some kind of suit made of leaves."

"Sounds strange," Nancy commented. "Did he talk to you?"

"Sort of," Bess said, "but we couldn't understand him." Nancy suggested that perhaps the man was speaking in his native Indian language.

"Probably," Bess replied, adding, "He didn't hurt us. In fact he gave us some lunch. He threw a handful of delicious nuts to us, then disappeared into the forest."

When the conversation finished, Nancy asked Old Joe if he knew who the giant Indian was.

"I'm not sure," her host answered, "but if he's who I think he is, the Indian is harmless. Evidently he has lived in the forest all his life. I remember hearing about him when I was a young man. The authorities tried to capture him but never could. Since he was harmless, they finally gave up."

George asked, "Did you ever catch a glimpse of him?"

"Not for many years," the elderly man replied.

George next asked the naturalist if any other Indians lived in the area. Old Joe shook his head.

George giggled. "Then maybe he doesn't belong here. Perhaps the spaceship dropped him off!"

Ned grinned. "So now we have a new kind of spaceman. An Unidentified Flying Indian!"

As the others laughed, Trixie bounded up to them with a large trout in her mouth.

"Good dog," Old Joe praised her. "I think there's enough food here for all of us. You won't have to get any more."

Ned took the fish. He cut off the head and tail and threw them away, then expertly slit the fish open and removed all the bones, then cut the rest of the trout into small pieces.

Soon the spit was put up and the fire started underneath it. Old Joe hooked the chunks of fish onto the spurs of the three-legged rig. The welcome aroma of cooking fish filled the air.

Up to now there had been a gentle breeze, but suddenly the wind blew hard, toppling over the spit and the fish. The burning wood scattered. Nancy quickly grabbed a nearby bucket of water and doused the remaining flames.

"Are we going to have a cyclone?" George asked, gazing at the darkened sky.

Old Joe looked worried. "I don't know," he answered, "but this is exactly what happened once before when the flying saucer appeared."

5

The Spying Stranger

The sky became more overcast and the wind blew stronger by the moment, whipping leaves off the trees. Everything that was not stationary was thrown helter-skelter.

Old Joe cried out, "Watch for a brilliant light in the sky!"

Every few seconds the campers gazed upward as they scurried around, trying to save what they could. The tripod had collapsed and scattered. The pieces of fish had sailed through the air and disappeared.

"The fire is spreading!" Dave exclaimed.

Quickly he and Burt stamped out bits of burning wood that had blown from the embers, while

Nancy and George rescued several handmade bird feeders from various trees.

In the meantime, Ned had gone to quiet the nervous horses, who were whinnying and stamping excitedly, trying desperately to break loose.

"Whoa there, Goalpost!" he commanded firmly.

The animal obeyed. This had a calming effect on the others until suddenly Nancy gasped.

"The light!" she exclaimed and pointed to the sky. "Here comes the flying saucer!"

The whirling object hurtled through the sky, its two headlights flashing brilliant beams across the treetops. Almost instantly the UFO disappeared from view, and the wind stopped blowing.

"Where did the ship go?" Nancy asked Old Joe.

"I reckon it landed in Dismal Swamp," he replied. "That's where the saucer went last time it came."

"Where's that?" the young detective questioned him.

The naturalist pointed. "The swamp is between this mountain and the next—way down in the valley." The other mountain, he noted, was called Teepeeskunk. "A long time ago a tribe of Indians lived over there. They used to catch skunks and sell the fur in town, so the natives gave the mountain that name."

The campers laughed.

37

"And I suppose Dismal Swamp is pretty dismal." George grinned.

"*Very* dismal," the elderly man replied. "No one ever goes near the place. It smells mighty bad. If you're planning to take a look at the mysterious flying saucer, you'd better wear a gas mask!"

Nancy held her nose and giggled. "I don't care what it smells like," she said. "I must go there and investigate. Otherwise, how will we know if the spacecraft really came from outer space?"

George said she wondered how Bess and Jan had gotten through the windstorm. "I think we should call them right now on the walkie-talkie."

Ned pulled it out of his backpack and tried to signal Bess and Jan. He pushed the buzzer button again and again, but there was no response.

"Maybe something happened to them," George remarked in a worried voice.

Nancy, too, was very concerned. "We must find them right away!" she said and turned to Old Joe. "I'm sorry to leave in such a hurry. I promise to come back soon to hear about your mystery and help you solve it."

"Thank you. There's no rush. The mystery has been waiting a long time."

Hal, a capable woodsman, offered to lead the search for his wife and Bess. "I can make excellent time alone. Just follow my trail," he directed. "I'll leave blue chalk marks on trees."

38

Old Joe said he certainly hoped the missing campers were all right. "Perhaps they found shelter from the wind inside a cave or among some trees," he suggested hopefully. "I'm sorry about lunch. But wait a minute. I'll give you all something to eat on the way."

He scooted into his cabin and returned in a few minutes, carrying handfuls of something wrapped in huge grape leaves. "I think you'll enjoy eating this pheasant meat I cured. I bagged the little fellow right here in front of the cabin."

The campers thanked him, then Hal trotted off on his horse. Before the others could catch up to him, he was out of sight. Apparently Hal had chosen a shortcut back to where Jan and Bess had been left.

The riders found themselves jumping over small fallen trees and splashing through rivulets. Although Hal's path was fairly visible, the group realized it was hard on the horses and stopped to rest.

Admitting she was as tired as her horse, George sighed. "I thought I was pretty tough," she said, "but this forest almost has me beat."

Burt laughed, tweaking her chin affectionately. "Coming from you that's quite an admission."

For a few moments no one had much to say. Finally, Ned stood up. "Everybody set?"

He led the way, stopping frequently to identify

Hal's trail. The blue chalk marks seemed rather faint and far apart as underbrush trampled by Hal's horse had begun to spring back.

When all of them were at last convinced that they were lost, Nancy noticed a small gouge on a tree. "This is new," she observed. "Maybe Hal ran out of chalk and made this nick as a marker."

Following the direction it indicated, the riders finally reached the spot above the river where they had left Bess and Jan. Hal was there, talking with them.

Nancy and George dismounted at once and ran up the short slope. Both girls cried out, "Bess, are you all right? The windstorm didn't injure you and Jan?"

Bess smiled weakly. "I wouldn't say I'm all right, but I feel better."

Hal suggested they leave their horses on some level ground he had found beyond the slope. While the boys took the animals there, Jan explained to Nancy and George that the strong wind and overcast sky had frightened both of them. "We were fearful we might be blown into that rocky stream so we decided to climb a little higher up the mountain. We found shelter in an overhang."

She said their horses were nervous but were all right.

"I'm so relieved," George said.

When the boys returned, Ned asked, "Is your walkie-talkie broken? We couldn't reach you."

Bess said they had not heard it. "I guess the wind made too much noise, or maybe the sound didn't carry into the overhang."

Ned explained that they hadn't tried until the wind died down. He examined the set and found a loose wire that he immediately reattached. He asked Nancy to try calling him. Now the buzzer worked perfectly.

Bess told the others that the Indian with the long black hair had spied on them again.

"This time he wasn't wearing the suit of leaves. He had on a short deerskin jacket and long pants made of the same material. I've decided he's rather nice-looking after all. I just wish he could speak English."

Dave pretended to be jealous. "I'm very glad the Indian doesn't," he muttered, causing a blush to creep over Bess's face.

"Oh, Dave," she said shyly.

Burt cleared his throat, equally embarrassed. "I wonder where the Indian comes from and where he hides out."

Hal replied, "Possibly he's a descendant of the Indians who used to live around here."

"You mean," Dave spoke up, "that the tribe lives

41

somewhere else now, but he has returned here to see where his forebears lived?"

Hal nodded.

"Maybe the guy's a hermit," Dave suggested. "You can't tell whether or not he understands English just because he won't speak it."

Burt concurred, adding, "He could be deaf and dumb."

"Could be," Bess agreed.

Jan had picked some delicious wild strawberries. As the campers sat on the ground to eat them, the conversation turned to the flying saucer. Nancy told Jan and Bess about their visit with Old Joe and his story of the spaceship landing in Dismal Swamp between the mountains.

George added quickly, "According to Old Joe the swamp smells horrible. Maybe it has gas in it."

"Then I'm going to keep away," Bess announced.

"Well, I'm not," Nancy said, "and the sooner I go, the sooner I can solve the mystery of the flying saucer."

"Where is Dismal Swamp?" Jan asked. "I never heard of it and I've been in this forest many times."

Nancy pointed in the direction that Old Joe had indicated. "I guess we'll have to return to our other campsite, then travel down the mountainside from there."

"It's too late in the day to go to the swamp now,"

Ned told her. "How about going early tomorrow morning?"

Nancy nodded. "But," she added, "suppose the flying saucer takes off in the meantime? We may miss an opportunity to solve the mystery."

"We'll just have to take that chance," he said.

Bess suggested, "Why don't a few of you start out now? I'll stay here until morning. I can't walk too far and I still don't feel up to riding a horse. Too many bruises," she added with a rueful smile.

"I know what you mean," Nancy said kindly. Undecided about what was best to do, she then appealed to Jan and Hal. "We're in your hands. You know more about this forest than we do. What do you advise?"

Since all their supplies were still with the pack-horses, the couple suggested they set up camp at the spot where they had left the two animals.

"That way we can all stick together tonight," Jan added.

Bess groaned.

Jan said quickly, "You won't have to walk a step if it bothers you. These husky boys can carry you. I only hope the horses and the food are safe."

Ned grinned. "Shall we draw lots?"

"Not on your life!" Dave replied. "I'll carry her alone."

"Piggyback?" Bess giggled.

When the group was ready to leave, Bess suddenly shrieked. The others whirled around and stared at her.

"*Now* what's wrong?" George asked, a little annoyed at a further delay.

Terrified, her cousin motioned toward the trees. "There he is again!" she said. "The Indian!"

All eyes turned toward the clump of trees. Indeed, the mysterious man was standing there, motionless, staring at them.

"Oh!" the campers gasped.

His right hand, held high, clasped a huge rock. Was he about to throw it at them?

6

Sign Language

The Indian stood quite still. He did not lower his upraised arm or throw the rock he held.

"He's weird," Bess whispered.

For a few seconds the campers continued to stare at him, fearful of his next move. He was muscular, and though the Emerson football players felt they could put up a strong battle, they wondered if he might defeat them by some unusual strategy.

Nancy was the first to make a suggestion. "Let's try to be friendly and approach him with our hands outstretched."

Bess was not so sure this was a good idea. "Suppose—suppose he's from outer space," she said. "There's no telling what magnetic power he might have. He could mesmerize all of us."

This struck George as a funny idea. She said, "Oh, sure, and a killing bolt of electricity may come shooting out from his body at any minute—z-z-z— look out!"

Burt muffled a chuckle, adding, "Do you think that's his spaceship down in the swamp? He looks too big to live in it."

Bess knew they were teasing her but ignored it. She had seen the Indian before the saucer arrived. Then a thought struck her: Maybe the spaceship came back for him. He might even be planning to kidnap us and take us away in it!

As the Indian continued to stare at the group, Dave glanced at Bess, as if reading her thoughts, and exclaimed, "Watch out! He may hypnotize you!"

Bess made a face at Dave, then said, "Okay, Nancy. Why don't you and Ned approach the man?"

The couple walked forward, slowly. Nancy held a shining gold disc on a chain which she had removed from her neck. Perhaps, she thought, the Indian would be interested in the necklace.

Inch by inch, she and Ned continued toward him. The Indian remained immobile. He stared at the jewelry but did not take it. Finally he let the rock drop to the ground.

Ned sighed in relief. "Maybe he intends to be friendly," he murmured.

47

As Nancy stepped closer, she smiled and said, "Hello."

The girl detective repeated the greeting several times as she and Ned came right up to the man. He still did not move, but just looked straight at them. Would he attack? The onlookers watched with bated breath.

Now Ned pointed to himself, saying over and over, "Ned. Ned. Ned."

Finally the Indian gave a slight smile and then pointed to Nancy. Ned complied with the sign language. "Nancy. Nancy."

Everyone was delighted and started to applaud, but Jan signaled for silence.

A hush fell over the group as the man pointed to himself and said, "Shoso."

The campers were thrilled. Again they wanted to clap, but Jan shook her head. She was afraid that loud applause might frighten the man away and send him racing off into the forest.

Now Shoso laid a finger gently on Ned and repeated his name several times. In turn, he and Nancy pointed at the Indian and said, "Shoso." He nodded and smiled broadly.

He looked up at the sky and said something unintelligible to them.

"What's he trying to tell us?" Ned asked Nancy.

The young sleuth admitted she was puzzled.

"Maybe he'll tell us some more in sign language."

48

Presently Shoso twirled quickly with his arms above his head. Still the couple looked puzzled. Shoso repeated the motion.

"I think I get it," Ned remarked. "He's trying to imitate the windstorm."

Nancy agreed. "But I just can't figure out his message."

Shoso seemed disappointed and thought a few seconds. Then he leaned down, put his hands on the ground, and galloped about. Suddenly he ran off a short distance into the trees.

Nancy snapped her fingers. "Ned, I think Shoso is trying to tell us something about our horses."

"We'll soon find out," he replied, "if we use some sign language of our own."

He leaned over the way Shoso had done and told Nancy to hop on his back as if she were riding a horse.

As Nancy did this, she laughed and said," I sure feel silly, but if it works, I don't mind."

By this time the other campers, no longer afraid of the Indian, began to roar with laughter.

"You two ought to join the circus," Burt called out.

George scoffed. "A kindergarten circus."

Ned and Nancy played their parts well, ignoring the jibes. Shoso nodded happily and pointed in the direction where the boys had left the horses.

"Something must have happened to them!

49

Maybe they've been injured!" Nancy exlaimed, jumping off Ned's back.

"Or perhaps they ran away," he replied. "We didn't tie them all. We let a few graze."

"Yes," Burt agreed. "They may have injured themselves being loose in this forest. I've noticed plenty of trailing vines."

"Don't say that," Bess pleaded. "I can't stand to see an animal hurt."

Without wasting another minute, all the campers and Shoso rushed toward the spot where the saddle horses had been left. *Two of them were gone!*

"Oh, what'll we do?" Bess wailed.

"I blame myself," Dave said. "I suggested we let some of the animals graze."

"We're all guilty," Burt added. "We didn't have to take your advice."

Nancy noticed with relief that her lovely Susan B was still there with Goalpost standing next to her. Unfortunately the horses Burt and Dave had been riding were missing. Hal suggested that possibly the animals had gone back to the original campsite.

Jan said, "I have a hunch they may have rejoined the packhorses."

"Oh, I hope you're right," Bess answered. "They have all the food and I'm starved."

Hal said that he was less concerned with their supplies. He hoped that the great wind and the blinding bright lights of the saucer had not frightened the packhorses so much that they yanked themselves loose from the tie ropes.

Although the campers had had little to eat that day, they knew their main job was to find the horses.

Shoso seemed to feel sorry for the group. He beckoned them to follow him. Burt and Dave rode double with George and Bess.

The Indian led them directly toward the campsite where they had left the packhorses. The route was much shorter than the one the group had taken that morning while heading for Old Joe's.

"Oh, thank you," Bess called to him, then remembered that he could not understand her words. He waved and disappeared from view.

Nancy and her friends rushed to the area where the packhorses had been tied. To everyone's dismay, the missing saddle horses were not there. Moreover, both packhorses were gone and so were the supplies!

7

Old Joe's Secret

"Four of our horses gone!" George exclaimed, sighing deeply.

"And all our food and clothes!" Bess moaned.

The campers were nonplussed. What were they going to do without them?

Hal remarked, "Judging from the frayed ropes, I'd say the animals went wild."

"Then there's no telling how far away they went," Nancy commented. "Maybe Shoso knows."

The Indian, however, was not in sight.

"He's the most elusive man I've ever met," Bess commented.

Nancy visualized the tall, erect figure stalking through the forest. Except for the deeper color of

Shoso's skin, his black hair and dark eyes, he was the same type of outdoorsman as Old Joe. The girl wondered if all naturalists were similar in stature.

Hal, in the meantime, was trying to reassure the campers about their horses. "Sometimes they return to their riders."

"That's right," Jan agreed. "We'll manage somehow. If Old Joe can subsist in this forest, so can we."

Nevertheless, Nancy was disappointed. "I was so hoping all of us could go to Dismal Swamp. After all, my main reason for coming here was to investigate the flying saucer. By now, it may have left."

"I doubt it," Ned remarked. "I'm sure we would have seen it take off."

Nancy was not so certain of this. Perhaps the mystery ship had unknown powers that allowed it to depart silently and invisibly.

"We'll get to the swamp somehow," Ned assured her.

They both looked for hoofprints to see which way the missing horses had gone. The search indicated that the pack animals and riding horses had run off in separate pairs. But the hoofprints of all four led to the bank of a small stream where the prints ended. Evidently the horses had walked through the water. It was growing too dark, however, to continue the hunt.

Jan said, "Let's fix a good meal. That will liven our spirits."

"Fix it out of what?" Bess asked.

"The forest," Jan replied. "I suggest we split up in couples and forage for food. In an hour I would bet we'll have a great dinner."

George laughed. "I'll feel like a foraging cow. *Moo moo.* Come on, Burt."

Jan asked Bess and Dave to stay nearby in case any of the horses came back. She smiled. "This time, please tie them."

"You bet," Dave promised, still upset about being partly responsible for the two runaway animals.

Hal and Jan went off in one direction, Nancy and Ned in another. To the young sleuth's delight, she discovered a huge patch of wild blueberries. "But what can I put them in?" she asked.

Ned pulled a large brown handkerchief out of his pocket, filled it, and tied the four corners together. Before the hour was up, the couple had gathered wild scallions and grapes as well.

When they joined their friends, Nancy and Ned were amazed at the variety of food the others had brought back. George and Burt, both mushroom experts, had collected and peeled a large quantity of mushrooms. Hal had chased and caught two rabbits which he had dressed and cut into pieces. He had skewered them onto a sturdy branch broken from a sapling and was now cooking the meat over a small fire Dave had built.

He and Bess had discovered a sassafras tree and chipped off pieces of bark which they mixed with water in a camper's abandoned canteen. Bess set it over the fire to brew into tea.

The meal was enjoyable and satisfying. The group discussed the day's events and finally the conversation turned to the missing horses.

George said, "I think we shouldn't dismiss the possibility that they were stolen."

The remark shocked everyone. If this were true, they might never get the horses back!

"But who would steal them?" Hal asked. "Very few people roam this mountain and I saw no footprints where the horses were tied. Besides, the frayed ropes seemed to indicate that they yanked themselves loose."

Bess asked, "Even if you found footprints, how could you tell that the person who made them had ridden away?"

Hal smiled. "You don't step over a horse's back. You hoist yourself up so you'd make more of a depression in the ground."

Bess giggled. "I guess I still have a lot to learn about horse detective work."

It was decided that Hal and Burt would start to hunt for the missing animals after breakfast the next morning. Hal said they would pick up the search where the hoofprints ended, ride through the stream, and try to find out where the horses had left the water.

"We'll take one of the walkie-talkies along," Burt said, "so you can let us know if any of the animals return, or if we find any of them we'll contact you."

Dave called, "Big game hunters, bring 'em back alive!"

"Shush!" said Bess. "You make me shiver."

That night the group collected pine needles and slept on refreshing beds of pine. The next morning, as daylight filtered down through the trees, Burt and Hal rode off. The campers who were awake wished them well.

"Watch out for wildcats and snakes!" Bess warned.

Burt laughed. "I dare any snake to try biting through these hiking boots."

The searchers were gone several hours but did not call in a report. Then suddenly George exclaimed, "Listen! I hear hoofbeats."

To be sure, she lay down and put her ear to the ground. "Yes, I hear at least two horses coming," she announced.

Everyone expected to see Hal and Burt, but to their amazement Old Joe appeared. He was leading the two lost saddle horses!

"How wonderful!" Nancy called out as she ran to pat them. "Old Joe, where did you find the horses?"

Her new friend grinned. "They came to my cabin. Guess they were hungry for something sweet and thought maybe I'd feed them, which I did. I gave them maple syrup candy. How'd they get away from here?"

Nancy and Ned told him the story, adding that Hal and Burt had gone off to look for the four runaways and the supplies.

Old Joe became philosophical. "Horses are funny creatures. You never can be sure what they're thinking. Sometimes they don't do anything unusual for a long, long time, then something will frighten them and they'll take off like they'd gone clean beserk."

As the campers crowded around the kindly man, Bess asked him if he would like a drink. "We have water and cold sassafras tea." She giggled and told about the campers' supper the night before.

The naturalist chuckled. "You'll be forest folk before you know it." Then he thanked them and said he had had a good breakfast. "But I brought you something. I keep a few hens in a cage near my cabin. Trixie stands guard, of course. She chases the wild animals away. I have some hard-boiled eggs for you."

As each person took an egg to eat, George remarked, "Too bad Burt and Hal aren't here. I think we should try to contact them on the walkie-talkie and tell them that the two saddle horses are back."

Nancy tried to signal the two searchers, but there was no response. Again and again she called in vain and finally asked Dave to examine the instrument.

"It seems okay," he reported. "I'm puzzled why Hal and Burt don't answer."

Old Joe spoke up. "Maybe your friends have gone out of range. Or maybe there are too many trees in the way of the signal."

When the old naturalist said he ought to be leaving, Nancy remembered that they had not yet heard about his mystery. She asked him about it, and he was delighted that she remembered.

He began by explaining that he and his parents lived in the city when he was a boy.

"However, my father was a great nature lover and used to bring me to this forest. I grew to love it as much as he did. After my mother's death my father and I came here more often. In fact, we once spent several months in the forest. That was when the mystery began.

"One day soon after we arrived, my father seemed worried. When I asked him what the trouble was, he told me that he was carrying a lot of money and valuable secret papers in his wallet.

"He said to me, 'Son, there's a man who is an enemy of mine. He would like nothing better than to get his hands on all of this. But I don't intend for him to do so. He must never learn the secret.'

"That night we were very tired and went to bed early. I slept soundly and when I woke up in the morning, my father was gone. At first I figured he was fishing or picking berries or maybe trying to catch a rabbit for some stew. But he did not come back for hours. I became alarmed.

"When he finally returned, I asked him where he had been. He said, 'Oh, just out for a long hike.'

"I was puzzled, but he didn't explain. Then suddenly one morning he announced that we were going back to the city. I asked him why and he told me he had business affairs to take care of.

"We never again came here together. Soon after returning to the city, he had a stroke. He wasn't able to walk, talk, or write. He lived only three more years.

"Just before he died he looked up at me and managed to say, 'F-forest. Mon— b-bur—'"

Spellbound, Old Joe's listeners now began to ask questions.

"Do you think your father was saying he had buried the money in this forest?" Nancy asked.

Old Joe nodded. "I came here many, many times and searched but never had any luck. Finally I decided to leave the city and live here permanently. This forest is more like home to me than any other place. All these years I've hoped to find the wallet and my father's great secret."

Nancy was tingling with excitement. If she could only find that wallet! The girl detective wondered, however, what condition it might be in.

I hope for Old Joe's sake it's intact, she thought. Aloud she suggested, "Let's talk about clues."

8

Pyramid of Rocks

All the campers had questions for Old Joe. Bess asked him, "Did your father have any special places in the forest he liked to go?"

"None that I recall," the naturalist replied. "He loved everything in it."

Ned inquired next if the elder Mr. Austin had any favorite trees.

After thinking over this question for a couple of minutes, Old Joe said, "The taller the tree, the more he admired it. I'd say perhaps the sky-reaching pines were his favorites."

"Then we'll examine those first," Nancy told him.

Jan said she wondered if Old Joe's father would have bothered to make it difficult for his son to find the wallet. "Perhaps your father had some cozy nook where he liked to spend time. Do you know of any?"

The old man told her the forest was full of wonderful small hideaways. "But so far as I know, there are no deep caves or overhangs of rock. I'm afraid I'm not much help to you."

Nancy was not discouraged. She asked Old Joe where he had looked for the wallet.

He smiled. "Hundreds of places," he told her, "but there are thousands more just waiting to be explored."

Nancy had a strong hunch that Mr. Austin had hidden his valuable wallet in a well-protected place. She suggested that Old Joe accompany the group on a new search.

"I'd certainly like to find that wallet," he said longingly. "Okay, I'll go with you."

Before the group had a chance to start off, however, they became aware of prolonged, frantic barking from Trixie. She had been left to guard the cabin.

"Uh-oh, trouble," Old Joe said worriedly. "Some unwanted visitor, I'll bet. I must go right back."

Nancy offered him one of the saddle horses. "Thanks a lot, but I can make better time on foot," Old Joe replied and hurried off.

Ned remarked, "I hate to see that old man go by

himself. I think I'll follow and see if I can help." Dave decided to go along with him.

As the barking continued, George said, "Ned and Dave may be gone a long time. Nancy, if you want to start the search, I'll be glad to go with you."

The young sleuth was eager to begin. She mentioned the idea to Jan and Bess, who felt that they should stay behind to guard the camp.

"We don't want any more trouble with the horses," Jan said.

"Please watch your step," Bess added.

Nancy and George took flashlights to explore the hollows of trees and other possible hiding places. They had been searching half an hour for Mr. Austin's wallet when George found a tree with a deep hole in the trunk.

Excitedly she flashed her light inside, then exclaimed, "Nancy, there's something at the bottom that looks like leather." She laid down the flashlight and reached in. Almost immediately George cried out in pain and yanked out her hand.

"What happened?" Nancy asked, running to George's side.

"Something bit me! Oh! Ow! It hurts!" George replied. She danced around, shaking her hand.

Quickly Nancy flashed her light on the tree. The beady-eyed head of a small snake was visible at the top of the hollow in the trunk. Blinded by the brightness, the reptile instantly slithered down into its den.

Was it a poisonous species? Nancy had no idea but decided not to take any chances. She whipped out a handkerchief and tied it tightly around George's wrist. Then she grabbed a sharp-pointed twig and made a tiny hole in the end of her friend's thumb. By now George's hand was swollen.

"I'm sorry I'll have to hurt you a little," Nancy told her friend, "but we must get that poison out before it spreads."

She hunted for a sharp stone. After cleaning it off with a green leaf, Nancy drew it across the end of George's thumb. Blood flowed out and, she hoped, all the poison as well. Soon the swelling subsided, and George said the severe ache was gone.

"Thanks a million, Nancy," she said gratefully. "I was really scared."

Now that George felt better, Nancy removed the tourniquet. "Do you want to continue the search?" the girl detective asked. "Or would you rather go back to camp for further first-aid treatment?"

George said she was feeling fine. "The bleeding has almost stopped. Maybe we can find a stream where I can bathe my thumb."

The two girls went on, looking intently for places where the Austin wallet might be hidden. Shortly they came to a babbling brook. While George swished her hand in the icy water, Nancy looked closely at the surroundings. She noticed an extremely tall pine tree, perhaps one admired by Old Joe's father. There was no opening in the trunk, however.

"Before we leave," she said to George, "I think I'll climb the tree and see if there's anything ahead."

Hugging the thick trunk, Nancy started to shinny up the tree. George merely looked on, chiding herself for her sore thumb, as Nancy climbed higher and higher. She was examining every inch of the main trunk and looking at each limb and branch. Nothing indicated that a wallet was hidden among them.

Finally at the top Nancy scanned the surrounding countryside and shouted down to George, "I can see Dismal Swamp from here. Oh, no, I can't believe it. The flying saucer is gone!"

"What a rotten break!" George said. "Let's hope it'll come back while we're still here."

Nancy felt miserable because she had lost her chance to see the flying saucer close up. Was her trip in vain?

I should have gone to the swamp as soon as the UFO landed, she thought. It was little consolation to her that the missing horses, Bess's accident, and darkness had compelled her and the others not to ride to the swamp.

Nancy descended the tree. When she reached the ground, George said, "Don't feel too bad. That flying saucer is bound to come back." She grinned. "I just had one of your hunches."

Nancy smiled wanly. "I hope it won't take a hundred million light years, though," she replied.

The girls walked on in silence. Despite their keen observance of many trees, short and tall, they found nothing in any of them to indicate a hiding place. George remarked that perhaps they would have to start digging.

Nancy nodded. "Next time we'll bring spades and picks. You know, George, we aren't very good woodsmen, not to have brought even a trowel!"

In a short while they came to another mountain stream, wider than the other and rocky. Water was rushing rapidly over the stones.

"Isn't that pretty?" George remarked. "It looks like a picture for a calendar!"

"It really does."

As Nancy stood on the bank, she noticed a pyramid of rocks about eighteen inches high in the middle of the stream.

"That's strange," she said. "I wonder what it's for. A marker of some sort?"

"A marker for what?" George asked.

Nancy shrugged and did not reply. She decided to investigate. She took off her hiking boots and socks and waded in. Not only had the stones been cemented together, she discovered, but the foundation reached a foot below the bed of the stream.

Very excited, Nancy asked herself: Could Old Joe's father have made this pyramid of rocks? Were his valuable wallet and secret papers inside?

9

The Black Deluge

Eager to communicate with Old Joe, but having no idea which direction to take to his cabin, Nancy and George decided to return to camp. Bess and Jan were glad to see them.

"We've been so worried about you. You were gone a long time," Jan said.

Suddenly Bess saw her cousin's finger. "George, whatever did you do to yourself?"

"A snake bit me," George replied, and she told them about her painful encounter.

Jan took a protective plastic finger from her first-aid kit and gave it to George to wear over her thumb. Then she said, "Now tell us about your search for Old Joe's treasure. Any luck?"

"Yes and no," Nancy responded.

She told Bess and Jan about the pyramid of rocks—a possible hiding place for the valuable wallet.

"It certainly sounds like a good guess," Bess remarked.

Knowing Jan was knowledgeable about woodlore, Nancy asked her if the pyramid might have been used for something else— perhaps to ward off some superstitious fear.

Jan shrugged. "Possibly. Or maybe someone erected it as an art object. It must have been pretty with the stream splashing around the pyramid."

"It was," George replied, then asked, "Jan, do you think it could have been a marker for fishermen?"

"Could be," Jan replied. "But I doubt that anyone would place one way out there in this wilderness."

Jan said she felt Nancy's guess was a likely one. "You should tell Old Joe soon."

Then Nancy described how she climbed the tree and learned that the flying saucer was gone.

"Did you hear it take off?"

"No."

"Feel any wind?"

"No."

"See any lights?"

"No."

69

"It's gone," Nancy said sadly. "I wonder if it will ever come back."

"Let's hope so," Bess said and gave Nancy a hug.

When Ned and Dave returned a short time later, Trixie was with them. She jumped around, delighted to see the campers.

Nancy asked what had happened at the naturalist's cabin. To her dismay she learned that the interior was almost wrecked.

"Old Joe found footprints of a bear that got in somehow," Dave reported. "Evidently Trixie couldn't scare him away. The bear ate most of the food he found. Besides that, he emptied the contents of a jar of honey and another of maple syrup.

"He made a shambles of the place," Dave went on. "We helped Old Joe fix things up as best we could. We left him repairing the cabin door which the bear apparently broke down. He must have been hungry."

Nancy and George related their adventures. When Nancy finished, she said, "I'll write a note to Old Joe about the pyramid of rocks and have Trixie deliver it. That might make him feel better."

Hastily she wrote down what the girls had discovered, then tied the note to a small piece of rope which she secured around the dog's neck.

"Take this right to Old Joe," Nancy instructed the

animal. "It's very important." Trixie understood and hurried off.

Without warning a brisk wind sprang up, and it started to rain. The campers put on their rain gear, wishing that the tents were with them and not with the missing packhorses.

"This is more than a rainfall," Bess remarked presently. "It's a deluge."

"A black deluge!" Dave added.

The campers huddled together under a maple tree as heavy drops of rain pelted through the spreading branches.

"I'm really beginning to worry about Hal and Burt," Jan remarked. "They're long overdue. And this weather won't help them any."

"Probably it's too dark for them to proceed," Nancy suggested.

"I hope they've found the horses," Bess remarked. "Then at least they could have something to eat and drink from the packs."

The conversation was interrupted when the forest suddenly lit up with a strange, bright glow.

"Maybe the flying saucer is coming back!" Nancy exclaimed. "Oh, I hope so!"

Ned offered to shinny up a tree to find out. Before he reached the top, however, the mysterious light was gone. Once again it was pitch dark. Gingerly he climbed down.

"This is positively spooky," Bess said.

Nancy stated firmly that she was not going to miss another chance to see the flying saucer.

"Ned," she asked, "are you game to go down to Dismal Swamp with me?"

"Sure," he replied. "Let's take two lantern searchlights with us."

Jan begged the couple not to walk. "You should ride, and take some candy in case you get hungry." Quickly she took two chocolate nut bars from her pack. "I almost forgot I had these," she said.

Nancy put a poncho over her rain gear while Ned took one out of his backpack. They swung the saddlebags across the animals' flanks, then put on the saddles and vaulted into them, covering the saddles as best they could with their ponchos.

"Keep close," Ned advised Nancy and nudged his horse to start off.

Nancy pulled her rain hood snugly forward and followed him. If only the rain would stop, she thought, we could make better time.

But it continued to beat hard, creating slippery craters of mud through the unbroken forest. When the riders reached a small clearing Goalpost picked up speed. He kicked up mud, splashing Susan B's forelegs and causing Nancy to rein in sharply. The mare, however, did not obey. She dug her hooves faster through the wet grass, sinking, then skidding and almost throwing Nancy out of the saddle.

"Whoa, Susan B!" the girl detective ordered. "Whoa!"

Ned heard Nancy's frantic cries. Instantly he swung Goalpost in her direction. The horse whinnied and stumbled toward Susan B. By now the mare was reluctantly under Nancy's control.

"Are you all right?" Ned shouted to Nancy.

"Yes, I'm fine," she replied, though still a bit shaken. "Let's go on."

As the couple started out again, a slight mist began to rise. Oh, no, Nancy thought. We don't need this. I must see the mystery spaceship.

It was only a short time later that she and Ned, shining their lantern searchlights ahead, picked up the dim outline of the flying saucer. It was resting in the center of the swamp in complete blackness.

"It really smells as horrible here as Old Joe said," Ned remarked. "Do you want to stay?"

"I sure do," Nancy replied. "Let's go the rest of the way on foot. We can leave the horses tied to trees up here."

By now the rain had almost stopped, although it continued to drip steadily from the trees. The ground in Dismal Swamp was spongy but passable. What almost stopped them, though, was the rank, gaseous odor. They wondered: How much of it was from the swamp and how much emanated from the flying saucer?

The craft itself was completely silent. Nancy

whispered, "If any creatures are aboard, they're either asleep or keeping quiet to avoid detection."

Ned agreed. "And we'd better watch our step so we don't run into any surprises."

He and Nancy sloshed through the swamp, shining their powerful searchlights on the mysterious craft. They walked around it, but saw no windows or doors.

"How does anybody get in or out of this saucer?" Ned asked. "It seems to be sealed up tight."

Nancy suggested that perhaps no one was aboard. "The craft may be operated by remote control," she said.

"Just the same," Ned remarked, "I'd like to go inside. Who knows what we'd find—maybe someone dead!"

Nancy was as curious as her companion to find out. "Let's pound on the hull," she said. "Maybe we'll get a response."

10

Space Trip

The rain had started to fall again and within seconds was coming down in torrents. Nancy and Ned, however, paid little attention to the deluge as they pounded on the flying saucer. Though they knocked until their knuckles were sore, no response came from the interior of the mysterious craft.

Finally Ned remarked, "Maybe we ought to try communicating by mathematical signals. Suppose I try a few that I've learned in my courses."

He took a key from his pocket and tapped it against the spaceship. First he indicated a simple triangle. There was no response. Next he tried a more complicated geometric formula. Again there was no answer.

Nancy was astounded that although the hull seemed to be made of metal, Ned's tapping made no metallic sound.

That's strange, she thought, and mentioned it to Ned.

"You're right," he agreed. "This ship has some kind of soundproof shell. Even if there's an intelligent being inside, it probably cannot hear my signals."

Wondering what the ship was made of, Ned tried to scrape the surface with his key. He was unable to chip off anything.

"This is incredible!" he exclaimed. "I'd like to know what kind of outer material this is. Possibly some substance from a distant planet."

He sighed, regretting he had not brought chemicals and testing equipment with him.

"Even if we could get in touch with some scientists nearby, they might not be able to reach here before the saucer takes off again."

He and Nancy speculated on the spaceship's source of energy.

"Whether it's programmed or remote-controlled," she remarked, "I'm inclined to think the ship is solar-powered. Perhaps the reason it's stuck here in the swamp is that we've had so much cloudy and rainy weather. The saucer may not have stored up enough solar energy to lift itself off the ground and back up into the air."

Ned said he wondered if the swamp itself exuded special gas that gave the ship buoyancy. "It smells bad enough around here to launch anything." He grinned. "I hope you and I don't suddenly take off!"

She laughed. "In this mud? No chance."

Suddenly aware that they were standing in a deep quagmire of mud and water, Ned asked Nancy if she were ready to go back to camp.

"Are you kidding?" she replied. "I want to see what happens! Whoever or whatever controls the ship may decide to leave suddenly."

"In that case," Ned said, "why don't we get those chocolate nut bars out of our saddlebags?"

"Good idea," Nancy agreed.

First, they retethered the animals so they could reach down to nibble on grass and roots, and even sleep until the couple was ready to leave. They removed their rations from the saddlebags and returned to the flying saucer where they ate the chocolate bars.

"Amazing how satisfying one large piece of candy can be," Nancy commented, leaning against the ship. She yawned.

"I feel better too," Ned remarked sleepily.

Suddenly Nancy felt the spaceship vibrate. She was startled and noticed a side door opening slowly. A mechanical hand reached outside and beckoned her and Ned to come aboard.

"Shall we go?" she whispered to him.

He did not reply. To her surprise, he walked, as if dazed, toward the doorway. She followed.

When they reached the spaceship, the mechanical hand helped them step inside, then retracted. The door slammed shut.

The interior of the craft was brightly illuminated but not by lights that the couple could see and there was no sign of anyone—human or humanoid.

The walls were lined with flashing lights and many kinds of buttons, gadgets, and tools. Some of them Nancy recognized as hammers, screwdrivers, and wrenches; others were totally unfamiliar to her.

She tried to ask Ned what some of the unusual ones were. To her utter astonishment, no sound came from her throat.

We must be in a void, she surmised, but we're not having any trouble breathing. How strange!

More baffling was the fact that all her rain gear was gone. Ned's was missing also. What had happened to it?

Did it evaporate? she asked herself, completely puzzled.

A feeling of fear crept over the young detective. Was she locked in the flying saucer? Were she and Ned about to be kidnapped by unseen space beings and taken away from the earth forever?

Ned, less frightened, began to examine the odd gadgets. None was labeled to give a clue to its use. Curious, he pushed a button on one wall. Sparks flew toward both him and Nancy, slightly scorching the backs of their hands.

Ouch! Nancy cried out, but again she made no audible sound.

The flying saucer vibrated convulsively and lifted from Dismal Swamp. Instantly it turned into a glass cage, climbing higher and higher at a terrific speed. Within seconds it soared above the mountaintop and spun into space.

Although the flying saucer twirled rapidly as it flew, Nancy and Ned managed to stand with ease. Strangely, they forgot their fears. Both of them tried to figure out what had caused the ship suddenly to become transparent. As they gazed outside, the misty sky changed to clear dark blue.

I'm—I'm getting dizzy, Nancy said, reaching for Ned's hand.

Of course, he did not hear her, and she noticed that his eyes were closing. He too was becoming dizzy. Was it from the height or the speed? In a moment he lost his balance.

Poor Ned! Nancy thought. I—I hope—

Both of them toppled onto the deck. As they fell, the flying saucer swirled jerkily. They realized that it was descending. Where was it about to land?

Nancy and Ned tried to stay awake and to get up and look outside to see what was happening. Their efforts were in vain. They could not move. Within seconds both of them blacked out!

11

Human Birds

Nancy and Ned had no way of knowing how long they were blacked out. When they became conscious, they were no longer in the flying saucer.

Instead, Nancy and Ned were lying on luscious green grass. The cloudless sky above them was a beautiful blue and the sun was shining.

The spaceship was not in sight. Where did it go? Nancy asked herself, feeling a chill sweep over her.

She realized it was very cold where they were. Nancy turned on her side to speak to Ned.

Where do you think we are? she asked him. To her utter dismay she knew that still no sound came from her throat.

Ned sat up and looked at Nancy. He asked with concern, Are you all right?

The identical phenomenon had happened to him. He was uttering a thought but not out loud. Suddenly Nancy became aware of what Ned was thinking. The two of them were communicating by thought waves!

This is fantastic! Nancy decided.

The couple stood up and gazed around. Again Nancy asked silently: Where do you think we are, Ned?

He shrugged and replied, Maybe we're somewhere on earth or marooned on another planet. My guess is we're out in space.

For a few moments she and Ned were terrified. They had enjoyed their lives on earth so much that they were not ready to say good-bye to parents, relatives, and friends. Nancy chided herself for being so eager to solve the mystery of the flying saucer in the first place.

Ned thought-waved to her: Don't panic! It may be nice here.

Alone and not knowing what else to do, the couple walked around, trying to warm up. The ground was spongy, and for the first time Nancy and Ned looked fully at each other. They were no longer wearing their own clothes!

Both of them had on tight-fitting military-type

pants and coats in a silver color, with a matching helmet that fit snugly. There were no buttons or zippers.

How does one get into and out of these clothes? Nancy wondered.

Ned did not speak, but he smiled broadly. Nancy could not hear him laugh, but understood what he was thinking.

This is weird! he was saying to her silently.

There was nothing in sight. No buildings, no trees, just a rubberlike expanse of green grass.

Nancy thought-waved to Ned: If we're not in heaven, but on some other planet, do you think the flying saucer will come back, pick us up, and take us home to earth?

Ned shrugged. I'm freezing in this silly costume, he responded. I feel like a person acting a part in some play, like *Earth Man Lost in Space*.

Nancy smiled. I do too, she told him.

The eerie silence had been nerve-racking. By chance the couple happened to look up at the sky. Not far above them a huge bird was flying. It looked like a combination eagle and airplane. As it passed overhead, the bird dipped its wings as if signaling to the couple below, then turned and repeated the gesture.

Was that a message for us? Nancy wondered, glancing at Ned.

At the same time she looked down at her feet. To her amazement the military-type silver pants ended in footgear that looked like bird's claws.

I can't believe it! Bird's feet! She was puzzled by the whole thing.

Ned grinned. Maybe we've become birds! Human birds! You look pretty nifty at that, he told Nancy.

Are we supposed to fly? she responded, still amazed.

Automatically she pictured Ned as a bird and looked at the back of his broad shoulders. There were two retracted wings!

We are supposed to fly! she thought-waved to him. That's what the bird was trying to tell us.

She pulled out the wings. They opened wide and in a few moments Ned was ready to fly.

Here I go! he announced.

Wait! Nancy pleaded. Don't leave me here alone. She felt her own back, found a pair of wings like Ned's, and asked him to pull hers out.

Nancy's wings spread apart too. She wondered what she should do next in order to fly.

Ned solved the problem by indicating that she should run her fingers through the ends of the wings and hold on. He helped her do this, then put his own fingers to his feathery gear.

Ready! Set! Go! he signaled.

The couple ran as fast as they could over the uneven ground stumbling several times, then began to pump their arms. Within seconds they were airborne! Nancy loved her newfound freedom, as she and Ned soared over the landscape.

Isn't this fun! she thought-waved to Ned who flew alongside her.

He replied, I wonder if I'd ever want to be an earthling again. Maybe it would be better to fly than to walk.

It dawned on Nancy that the two of them were moving at an incredible speed. She expected her arms to tire, but they had no feeling in them.

She pumped her wings a little harder and gathered speed. Strange! She did not feel wind rushing across her face. There was no sensation of any kind.

This is really contrary to everything I learned in science, she thought. Ned nodded that he, too, was puzzled.

After they flew without seeing any sign of life, they wondered what kind of creatures might be able to live in this environment. The place was entirely unpolluted.

Nancy smiled. People at home would like it here. There's no smoke, no streams of water containing trash, no debris or poisonous chemicals.

Ned thought-waved to her, If anyone does live here, how do they survive? Nothing at all seems to be growing here except grass.

His flying companion speculated, Maybe it's a planet of intelligent birds. But what do they live on? Everything needs air, food, and water.

Ned suggested with a grin that maybe the birds imported it all in capsules from another planet.

Nancy giggled at this idea. Bird importers!

After a long flight, the couple finally saw a cluster of buildings ahead. Was it a settlement?

They're all shaped like flying saucers, she remarked, and Ned nodded.

Surely somebody would be around. But as the two friends flew over the extensive terrain, there was no sign of movement anywhere in the city.

After flying some distance out of the area, the travelers came to a large section of green grass. Ned thought-waved to Nancy, Let's go down. I'm getting tired of flying.

I am too. Can you help me retract my wings?

Ned drew alongside her, reached out to hunt for some kind of gadget on her back. He could find none. Nancy also tried to locate a similar device on Ned's wings, but she, too, came up with nothing.

The couple panicked. Were they doomed to fly throughout eternity?

Nancy tried to overcome her fear. It suddenly dawned on her that maybe the wings were thought-controlled.

She closed her eyes tightly and concentrated on Ned. Suddenly his wings retracted. He plummeted to the ground.

Within seconds she had drifted beyond him. She tried to retract her own wings but could not.

I must do something—and fast! she told herself. I mustn't fail!

Nancy pleaded for Ned to help her. He anwered, Turn around and fly back toward me.

Nancy dipped her left wing but found herself flying in a circle. Next she tried to stop by lifting the wings so they were parallel to each other. The flying girl wobbled uncontrollably. Was she going to fall?

Again Nancy was headed away from Ned and flying alone very, very fast!

12

Where? What?

Nancy was desperate as she soared above the uninhabited terrain. How could she retract her wings and glide back safely to the ground?

I mustn't let myself be stranded out here, she thought anxiously. I have to get back to Ned. But how? Oh, this is the worst thing that has ever happened to me!

Once more the young sleuth tried to gain control of the situation. By maneuvering carefully, dipping one wing, then the other, she managed by an erratic course to turn herself around. Relieved, she headed in Ned's direction.

I hope he's safe. Nancy sighed. He has to be. Finally she spotted glints of silver far below her.

There he is! Nancy thought excitedly.

She sent him a mental message: Please help me get down! My wings are out of control. Even when I stop pumping my arms, I keep going.

In reply, Ned suggested that Nancy hold her arms back as far as possible. She complied and gradually began to descend. As she neared the ground, Ned caught hold of her to break her fall and pinned her down to keep her from taking off again.

The entire experience had exhausted Nancy. The sky, the landscape, even Ned began to spin in front of her eyes. "Ned, Ned, I'm afraid I—" she mumbled before blacking out.

It was some time later when Nancy awoke. To her astonishment, the girl detective was lying in Dismal Swamp of Shawniegunk Mountain, U.S.A. Ned was nearby. He too was regaining consciousness and stirred slightly.

Through hazy vision Nancy thought she saw the Indian Shoso kneeling beside her. Then she became aware that there was a large leaf in her mouth. It tasted bitter.

How did this get in my mouth and why? she wondered.

As Nancy started to take it out, Shoso shook his head vehemently and pushed the leaf back inside. He pretended to chew, indicating she should do the

same. Too groggy to refuse, Nancy obeyed and was surprised that she soon felt much better. Now she sat up and looked around her. The flying saucer was gone!

Had the spaceship brought Nancy and Ned back to the swamp, then flown off again? Maybe Shoso could tell them.

Using sign language, she asked him if he had seen it leave. He held out his arms in a circle, then pointed to the sky. Next, he fluttered his fingers up and down, implying that rain or rays of some sort had begun to fall. Shoso pointed to the sky again, then finished by making another circle with his arms.

I believe Shoso is trying to tell me that it rained hard, but after the sun came out the flying saucer took off.

Nancy looked up at the sky. The sun was shining brightly and it was hot. The swamp was steaming and the rank, nauseating odor was stronger than ever.

Ned sat up. He was chewing a leaf. As he swallowed it, the couple looked at each other and smiled.

"What an incredible trip we had!" Nancy exclaimed.

"We?" Ned gulped. "You weren't with me."

"Part of the time I was," she told him.

The boy shook his head. "You must have been dreaming," he said.

Nancy's blackout scene was so vivid in her mind she found it hard to believe him. She glanced at the backs of Ned's hands: neither was scorched. Nancy looked down at her own; they were all right, too.

"But I was so sure—"

The girl detective next noticed that she and Ned had on their rain gear—their own clothes! What happened to the fantastic bird-flying suits they had worn? And what about the grotesque bird's claws that had covered their feet?

Nancy shook her head and laughed. "Ned, I've just awakened from the most incredible dream I've ever had. I still can't believe that it was all my imagination."

"Tell me about it," Ned requested.

As she related the story, Nancy kept including him in it. He roared with laughter when she described the two of them in flight through the windless air of an unknown planet.

"Human birds, eh?"

However, he sobered when she mentioned that at one point she wondered if they had died and gone to heaven.

"Too bad you didn't bring back a pair of angel wings," he teased.

She chuckled and took a deep breath. He told

her that in his dream he had not left the forest. "But I became some kind of knight, slashing a sword at wild beasts. I knew what some of them were, but others looked strange—prehistoric."

Nancy and Ned decided that gas from either the swamp or the flying saucer had put them to sleep.

"It's a shame the flying saucer left before we had a chance to investigate it more thoroughly," Nancy remarked.

"It may come back," Ned told her, trying to cheer up the young sleuth. "I'd say the ship was in some kind of trouble when it landed. Otherwise, it wouldn't have stayed so long and put up with our hammering, trying to learn its secret."

"Don't forget that the ship may have been programmed. Maybe it landed and took off exactly when it was supposed to," Nancy suggested. "Who knows what its owners planned to do with it?"

Ned suggested that Shoso might know when it left. "Let's ask him."

The couple stood up and looked around. The Indian was not in sight. They called his name again and again, but he did not appear.

"Too bad," Ned commented. "Now what?"

Nancy suggested that they search for any evidence that the ship might have left. In the center of the swamp was a badly scorched depression which she and Ned noticed for the first time.

Nancy said, "When the flying saucer took off, its antigravity rays may have been so hot they burned the ground. Let's dig up a little of the soil and take it back to camp for a lab analysis."

"Good idea," Ned replied.

Nancy headed for the saddlebags on her horse. Susan B, she was relieved to find, was safe. Apparently the gas from the swamp or flying saucer had not reached the animals. She hugged Susan B and patted Goalpost.

"I'm glad nothing hapened to you," Nancy said affectionately and unfastened one of her saddlebags. She took out a trowel and a small plastic bag.

When Nancy returned to the swamp, Ned dug up a chunk of scorched soil and dumped it into the bag, which Nancy held open. Then she took the mysterious sample back to Susan B, placed it in the saddlebag, and fastened the flap tightly.

She said to Ned, who had followed her up the slope, "Wouldn't it be wonderful if chemists found something in this sample different from anything known on earth?"

"Boy, would it ever!" Ned replied. "It might revolutionize our whole concept of the universe!"

The couple mounted their horses and set off for camp. They had not gone far, when suddenly Susan B sunfished.

"Easy, girl!" Nancy cried out.

She barely managed to control the horse and stay astride. The saddlebags nearly fell off as the animal dropped down on her forelegs and then lay down on one side. Nancy jumped off. The horse kicked viciously, trying to reach the saddlebag containing the soil sample.

"What's the matter with her?" Ned asked, puzzled by the strange behavior.

Furiously the horse kicked her hooves as the couple watched, helpless.

"She seems to be trying to get at that saddlebag," Nancy observed, keeping a safe distance from the animal. "I'm sure something inside it is bothering her. But what?"

13

A Discovery

Ned jumped from his horse and hurried forward to help Nancy and the distressed mare.

"Thank goodness you weren't hurt, Nancy," he said. "Susan B is really acting up."

"The poor thing's beside herself," Nancy said.

The riders urged the animal to stand up. Then quickly they pulled off the saddlebag.

"Look!" Nancy exclaimed, staring at the horse's flank." Her skin is badly scorched here."

Quickly they flipped over the saddlebag. A large hole had burned through the leather.

"It must have come from the sod we dug up," the young sleuth remarked, alarmed. "Oh, Ned, maybe it's radioactive!"

She unbuckled the saddlebag and dumped the contents on the ground. The plastic bag containing the sample also had burned through.

Nancy and Ned stared at each other as the same thought ran through their minds: Susan B might be contaminated!

"Ned, you and I might be contaminated, too!" Nancy cried out in alarm.

Other articles in the bag did not appear to be damaged, including a jar of healing salve. Quickly Nancy dipped her finger into the ointment and spread a generous amount over the scorched area on Susan B's flank.

She remarked, "Ned, if we've been exposed to radioactive material, I wish this salve alone could cure us. What do you think we should do?"

Ned advised that they bury the chunk of scorched earth, the saddle, and the saddlebag and everything in it.

"Good idea," Nancy agreed.

Using the trowel, Ned dug a deep hole. Nancy dropped in the suspect pieces one by one. After piling dirt over them and marking the spot with a heap of twigs, the campers started off again.

Nancy sat behind Ned on Goalpost, her own horse's lead rope in hand. "As soon as we get to town," she said, "I think we'd better get in touch with some scientists and a vet. Why don't we phone my dad? He might be able to fly up here right away and bring help with him."

"Good thinking," Ned replied.

When the couple rode into camp, they were bombarded with questions by their friends. Before they could answer them, Hal and Burt arrived, leading the two missing packhorses.

"I'm so glad you're back!" Jan exclaimed. "Now we have all the horses again."

"But mine is injured," Nancy announced and told the fantastic story of what happened to her and Ned.

The possibility that she and Ned might be contaminated by radioactive material really horrified everyone.

Dave spoke up. "It's not catching, thank goodness, so we don't have to isolate you two. But we shouldn't use any of the same eating utensils."

Jan offered to ride into town with Nancy, Ned, and the injured mare. "Nancy, you can take one of the other riding horses."

The group ate a light meal, then started off. When they reached the little town at the foot of the mountain, Nancy called her father and told him the amazing story.

"What!" he exclaimed. "Tell me everything. How are you and Ned?"

Nancy gave him all the details, and he replied, "I'll get a plane and scientists and doctors to come up there at once. I'll be with them. Wait right there for us. If we're going to be delayed, I'll phone you in about an hour."

Mr. Drew took the number of the telephone Nancy was using. "By the way, dear," he said, "an excited young woman phoned and wants you to solve a mystery for her. Something about strange identities. I told her you're tied up on another mystery right now, but she begged me to get in touch with you and call her back. What shall I tell her?"

"Oh, I wish I could help." Nancy sighed. "Dad, why don't you suggest she contact our friends the Dana Girls? They're great at solving mysteries."

"I'll do that," Mr. Drew promised. Then he hung up the phone, and Nancy returned to Ned and Jan.

"We're going to have a fairly long wait," she remarked. "Can we take Susan B to a vet?"

Jan nodded. "Follow me."

The three walked to the office-hospital of Dr. Doyle. Fortunately, he was able to examine the stricken animal at once. Nancy told him about the swamp but did not mention the flying saucer. This was to remain a secret until the mystery was solved.

"We thought it might be interesting to have the soil analyzed," she said, "and decided to bring some of it back to camp. The sample was so hot it burned a hole through my saddlebag and injured my horse's flank. I put salve on it." Nancy gave Dr. Doyle the name of the ointment.

"Quick thinking," the veterinarian complimented her.

"What worries us in particular is that part of

Dismal Swamp may be contaminated by radiation and could have affected Susan B. My father is flying here with some chemists to analyze it."

Dr. Doyle looked surprised. "How could Dismal Swamp become contaminated?" he inquired, puzzled.

Nancy shrugged. After the veterinarian had examined Susan B's wound, he said, "I suggest you leave the horse here. This is a pretty bad burn ."

"All right," Jan said, adding that the animal had been rented in town. "But our group will be responsible for your fee."

Before Nancy left the office, she put her arms around the horse that she had grown to love. She whispered in Susan B's ear, "I'm so sorry I got you into this. I hope you'll be okay soon."

After they left, Jan said they would need to rent horses for the new arrivals, a replacement horse for Nancy, and two more packhorses to carry whatever equipment the party might bring. "And we'll buy a lot of food to take back to camp," she added.

By the time the extra horses were collected and all purchases made, Nancy and her friends heard the whir of a helicopter overhead. It did not go to the airfield, but came down in a field on the outskirts of town. Nancy, Ned, and Jan hurried to meet its passengers.

As soon as Nancy saw her father step out of the copter, she ran ahead of the others. Then she stopped short. If I'm contaminated, perhaps I should not kiss him, the girl thought. She blew a kiss from a distance. He laughed, came up, and gave her a hug.

"Let's not be overanxious about this," he said. "I've brought two doctors and two scientists with me. Others will arrive later. Right now the doctors are going to test you and Ned for radioactivity."

After introductions had been made, one of the doctors took from his bag a strange-looking instrument with all sorts of dials and indicators on its face. He held the end of a tube with a knob against Nancy's heart, lungs, and the back of her neck. Was he testing her brain?

"So far everything is negative," Dr. Caffrey reported. "Now, young man," he said, "it's your turn."

Ned, too, was pronounced all right. The doctor shook his head and remarked, "You're lucky." He put away his instruments and the group stowed their gear on the packhorses and set off for camp. They had barely started when Nancy rode up beside Jan and asked if she would please stop the string of riders.

Without questioning Nancy's reason, the leader called out, "Halt!"

Everyone reined in. Nancy said, "It just occurred to me that perhaps we should have Dr. Caffrey examine Susan B for contamination. After all, she was burned by the sod in the swamp, but Ned and

I didn't touch it with our bare hands, or get any mud from the scorched area on us."

"You're right," Jan agreed and called out to the doctor, "Can you give the horse with the burn a radioactive test?"

"Sure. Glad to."

Jan told the others, "Wait here for us. Nancy and I will ride to the vet's and have Susan B examined for contamination."

Everyone agreed to the plan and the three riders galloped off. Twenty minutes later they were back.

"The horse is okay," the doctor reported. "She has a nasty burn but no contamination symptoms. Nevertheless, I think that swamp definitely should be investigated."

"It will be," Nancy said, then added, "Let's go!"

The riders urged their horses up the mountain. When they arrived at camp, their anxious friends were delighted to hear the results of the tests. The newcomers were introduced and they all sat down to a hot supper.

Nancy and Ned asked Hal and Burt to explain how they had found the lost packhorses. According to the boys it had not been easy, but after a fruitless search, they had finally heard a whinny.

"One horse caught a front hoof in a bear trap," Hal said. "Of course he couldn't move, but we managed to get the trap off. Fortunately it had snapped around the colt's hoof, not in it, so he wasn't really injured."

Now it was Nancy and Ned's turn to relate their adventure. The doctors and scientists laughed.

Mr. Drew chuckled also. "I like the part where you two couldn't talk, but were able to communicate by thought waves. From now on I'll have to be careful what I think!"

"That's right, Dad," Nancy said with a mischievous wink.

Early next morning Nancy was awakened by a barking dog. That sounds like Trixie, she told herself, and jumped out of her sleeping bag. She slipped on her jeans over her pajamas and went outside.

George joined her as Trixie bounded into camp and rushed up to the girls.

"Trixie has a note tied to the rope around her neck!" George exlaimed.

Quickly she removed the message and opened it for her and Nancy to read.

14

A Valuable Clue

The two girls read the note aloud. It had been signed by Old Joe.

> Dear Nancy and Friends,
> I am still amazed by your finding the stone pyramid. It was a valuable clue. I went to the brook myself; below the waterline I found a marker, and to my amazement my father's initials were on it.

George exclaimed, "How wonderful!" She and Nancy read on:

> There was also an arrow on the marker. I followed its direction for some distance, then I injured my foot.

"What a shame!" Nancy remarked. "I hope it's not bad. Well, let's see what else Old Joe has written."

The note continued:

I knew I had to give up the search. It was only with great difficulty that I got back to my cabin. Now I have a favor to ask of you: Would you young people like to take up the search?

Nancy and George looked at each other, then grinned. George said, "Would we!"

"It's an exciting challenge," Nancy admitted, but added, "You know that we won't be able to go immediately."

"Why not?" George asked, eager to take up the hunt.

Nancy reminded her that more scientists were arriving and would probably want to ask questions of the campers, especially Nancy and Ned. "I think I should stay here."

George agreed. "Have you any idea when the rest of the experts are coming?"

Nancy shook her head no. "I'm sure it'll be soon. In the meantime, I ought to get some paper and a pencil and answer Old Joe."

In her reply she said that the young sleuths would do their best to find out where the arrow led.

Then she added:

But I will have to wait at camp a little while before starting. Some scientists are coming here to examine Dismal Swamp. Ned and I discovered it was scorched, apparently by the flying saucer. Incidentally, I'm sorry to say that the ship took off again.

She explained briefly what had happened to her and Ned and how Shoso had put restorative leaves in their mouths.

Old Joe, do you have any idea what those leaves are?

She signed the note, attached it to the dog's rope collar, and said, "Trixie, take this back to your master." The dog bounded off.

Soon afterward the other campers were awake. Nancy showed the note to Bess and Jan.

"Oh! The poor man!" Bess said. "I'd like to help him. Would somebody go over to his cabin with me?"

Jan offered to accompany her. "I'll pack some medical supplies and see what I can do to relieve Old Joe's pain."

For a few minutes Jan and the girls discussed whether they should ask one of the visiting doctors to go along.

"They would probably prefer to wait for the rest

of the scientists to investigate Dismal Swamp to-gether," Nancy said.

As Bess and Jan gathered supplies, the young detective asked her father to take a walk with her. When they were out of hearing range of the other campers, he asked, "What's on your mind, dear?"

"I was wondering if we should notify the FBI or another top-secret agency about the flying saucer. I have a strong hunch the ship will come back. Wouldn't it be wonderful if the U.S. could capture it?"

Mr. Drew stared at his daughter, then grinned. "It's a great idea but a big order. We don't know if the saucer is from outer space, or the property of some rival country that's spying on us. In any case, I'll ride into town and make some phone calls."

He and Nancy walked back to camp. They learned that Bess had packed some food for Old Joe. As soon as breakfast was over, she and Jan set off for the naturalist's cabin.

On the way Shoso suddenly appeared. He was muttering unintelligibly. Was he trying to tell them something?

Jan said, "I have an idea he's speaking his Indian dialect. It's so strange because, as you know, there are no Indians in this vicinity anymore."

"Maybe he's a wanderer," Bess suggested.

"But Indians usually stay in bands or tribes," Jan countered.

Shoso was gesticulating with his arms, and finally motioned the two campers to follow him.

"Shall we do it?" Bess asked her companion.

"Oh, sure. Why not?" Jan replied. "Besides, I'm curious to find out where he wants to take us."

Shoso seemed to know every inch of the forest. To their surprise he led them to Old Joe's cabin by a completely different route.

"It's about half the distance," Jan remarked. "I hope we can find our way back to camp the same way."

The Indian dropped behind Jan and Bess. Before they could turn to thank him he had, as usual, disappeared.

Bess remarked dreamily, "If I hadn't seen Shoso in person, I'd think he's a spirit. He appears and vanishes so fast, it's like magic."

Jan laughed and said that was a good description of the Indian. They now approached the open cabin door and called inside.

"Come in!" Old Joe responded.

He was sitting up in bed with a huge bandage wrapped around his injured foot.

"Hello," he said. "Isn't this a great way for a forest dweller to treat himself? And I'd just started on an exciting hunt to solve my mystery."

Bess smiled and shook hands with him. "Everybody has an accident once in a while," she said soothingly.

Jan told him she was a nurse. "What have you been doing for yourself, Old Joe?"

"Don't you girls smell what's cooking in my fireplace?"

Jan and Bess nodded. The delicious aroma of pine filled the room. Jan peered into the pot where a combination of pine bark, sap from the tree, and crushed pine needles was brewing. It had cooked down to a thick, jellylike consistency. Old Joe said he had put this mixture on his foot and ankle, then bandaged the whole thing.

Jan smiled. "I couldn't have done better myself. Pine is one of the most healing remedies that exist. I remember an old saying—if anything ails you, go into the forest and lie on a bed of pine needles. It will cure colds or any other type of respiratory disorder. Moreover, it will pep up circulation, and this in turn can cure almost any type of illness a person has except, of course, broken bones."

The naturalist bobbed his head. "I learned the same thing from my father. And let me tell you, it works."

Old Joe brought up Nancy's note. "Please tell Nancy that I don't know what kind of leaves Shoso gave her and Ned. But if you see the Indian ask him to show you where he got the leaves, and give a few to the doctors to analyze."

Bess and Jan prepared the food they had brought and Old Joe accepted it gratefully. When he'd almost finished eating, he called to Trixie.

With a twinkle in his eye, Old Joe said to his visitors, "Don't you think she deserves a little of this good food for doing my errand so promptly?"

"We sure do," Bess agreed. The dog lapped up the remains of the canned beef and wagged her tail in appreciation.

The callers said good-bye and started for camp. Bess and Jan followed the trail which Shoso had shown them. Halfway along they saw the Indian again. He stood before them, arms crossed. First Jan, then Bess, asked him about the restorative leaves. What plant or tree did they come from and could he give them some more? Shoso stared at them blankly. He didn't understand a word.

"I'll try sign language," Bess said hopefully and started a little pantomime for him to watch.

First she raised her arms then flapped them to show that something was coming down from the sky.

She said to Jan, "I hope Shoso won't think that it's a bird. But how do I indicate a flying saucer descending?"

"I haven't the faintest idea," Jan replied.

The Indian watched Bess very carefully as she lay down on the ground and closed her eyes, pretending to be asleep.

Jan caught on to the little act. She pulled a leaf

off a nearby aspen tree and put it in Bess's mouth. The girl chewed it and opened her eyes. She stood up and looked hopefully at Shoso. If only she could get her urgent message across!

Apparently the Indian understood. He nodded and picked several of the same leaves. Then Shoso gave Bess a faint smile and hurried off through the forest.

Jan remarked, "You're quite an actress, Bess. He caught on fast."

"I only hope my message was clear to him," the pantomimist replied. Then she giggled. "Imagine playing charades out here in the forest with an Indian who doesn't speak a word of English!"

Jan grinned. "There's always a first time for everything."

Bess laughed, then she and Jan continued their ride. As they neared their campsite, they heard the loud noise of a helicopter. They looked up but saw nothing. Reining in, they paused to listen and kept their eyes skyward.

"I wonder if the pilot's trying to find us," Jan said. "That certainly would be difficult in this dense forest."

"You mean," Bess asked, "that if he's trying to locate us, he'll land at the foot of the mountain and walk or ride up here to talk to us?"

"Probably," Jan replied.

"What do you suppose he wants?" Bess asked.

"Listen!" Jan ordered suddenly. "The copter sounds as if it's in trouble."

"Oh, I hope not," Bess gasped in fright as the engine sputtered, died, then caught again. Within seconds it repeated the worrisome sound. "It would be dreadful for that poor pilot to crash in the forest!"

15

Lab in the Forest

The helicopter continued to make strange, faltering noises over the camp. Everyone on the ground was afraid it would crash on top of them.

"Why doesn't the pilot try to fly away? Surely he must see us," George complained.

Burt said, "Maybe I can communicate with the pilot by walkie-talkie." He tried to tune in but had no success. "The pilot can't pick up our wavelength, I guess," he said. "Too bad."

The craft dipped and rose, made a large sweeping circle, then flew back over the camp. Again Burt attempted to make contact. Finally he managed to get a faint response. "Come in whoever you are."

"I think I have him!" Burt exclaimed. He yelled

into the speaker, "Standing by in the forest below. Are you in trouble? Over."

"No, but I'm glad I contacted you. We have permission to land in the forest, but can't find a place. Any suggestions?"

Nancy, who had been listening, now spoke up. "Ask them how much room the copter needs."

"Not much," the pilot answered when Burt questioned him. "If we send tools down, can you cut some small trees to make space for us?"

Burt consulted the other boys and the scientists in the group.

"We can do it, but it won't be too smooth," Ned warned.

Burt relayed this to the pilot who said he would manage. "I'll make sure we avoid any leftover tree stumps."

Ned and the men gathered in a small clearing between clumps of trees and bushes. The copter hung overhead and lowered bags on a rope cable. After several of them had reached the ground, the cable was pulled up. The copter circled again.

The bags were opened and axes, saws, and other equipment taken out. The men divided into teams to tackle the saplings.

"Can't we girls do something?" Nancy asked.

Mr. Drew suggested that they pull up the bushes while the men worked on the trees. Soon the stillness of the forest was broken by the chopping sound of axes, the crash of small trees, and the buzz of saws as stumps were cut to the ground.

Whenever a heavier sapling needed to be removed, the men sliced off the branches for the girls to lug away, then either dragged the trunks beyond the immediate area or quickly sawed them into lengths that were easier to carry. Within a short time a landing area was ready for the copter.

As soon as it settled down, men poured from the doorway. First they introduced themselves to Mr. Drew, who in turn presented Jan, Hal, and all the young people.

Among the new arrivals were a botanist, a zoologist, three chemists, and two aerospace experts.

"This copter is not a standard model," said Dr. Halpern, one of the chemists. "It's really a flying lab. We wanted to park it as close to Dismal Swamp as possible."

Dave remarked, "I guess you don't often land in a forest."

"That's for sure." Dr. Halpern nodded, smiling. "What we have ahead of us are perhaps the most unusual experiments we've ever undertaken."

The men brought their own camping equipment and set up near their lab. When they finished, Dr. Halpern asked Nancy and Ned to tell them about their amazing adventure, including their dreams. The couple took turns filling in the details.

When they mentioned the effect of the restorative leaves that Shoso had fed them, Bess spoke up. "He's bringing us more. At least I think so."

The scientists were intrigued. "We'll analyze them," Dr. Halpern said promptly.

"I hope Shoso brings them soon." Bess sighed.

The newcomers were ready to go to Dismal Swamp. They brought masks and heavy gauntlets which they slung over their shoulders. A few carried trowels, others spades, and the rest, acid-proof bags. They borrowed available horses.

To Nancy and the others who stayed behind it seemed like hours before the group returned, but in fact, they were not gone long. As soon as they reappeared, however, all but one of them went to their laboratory to analyze the scorched sod.

One young man stopped long enough to say to Nancy, "You sure were right about the horrible odor from the swamp. I'm glad we had gas masks. I'll take my dreams in more pleasant surroundings!" He hurried after his co-workers.

The young sleuths, together with Mr. Drew, waited impatiently to hear the results of the tests. It was more than an hour later that the scientists rejoined the campers.

Dr. Halpern said, "I assume all of you are eager to know what we found. Frankly we have divided opinions. Some of us think the swamp produced the acid. Others feel the UFO left the acid which may have scorched one area of the swamp."

116

Nancy asked, "Have you decided yet what the chemical is?"

Dr. Halpern said that the scientists were still puzzled. "All I can tell you is that we've determined it is a strong, nonflammable acid, but very penetrating. One question is, if the flying saucer is responsible, did the acid come from some other planet?"

Dr. York, another scientist, spoke up. "If it's from Dismal Swamp itself, then we have quite a chemical mystery on our hands. To my knowledge, this acid is not found in such concentrated form anywhere else in the world."

The discussion turned to the possibility that the flying saucer sprayed the acid as it took off. Nancy and Ned reminded the men that they were overcome by the fumes before the saucer left.

"That does complicate the matter," Dr. Halpern admitted. "Well, we have many more experiments to make. I hope we come up with some definite answers soon."

Dr. Caffrey, who arrived with Mr. Drew, told the other scientists that he had tested Nancy and Ned for contamination by radiation. "Thank goodness, I found no sign of it," he declared.

Dr. Halpern asked if Dr. Caffrey would mind repeating the radiation test. "I'd like to see how your machine operates."

As before, Nancy was given a clean bill of health.

Ned was about to enter the tent where the test was being held, when he called out, "Do you expect sparks to fly from my head?"

The others laughed. "Not only sparks," Dave replied, "but a pair of antennas!"

When Ned and the doctor failed to appear within a reasonable time, the campers became anxious. Had Dr. Caffrey found something this time?

Nancy felt that she could not wait any longer for an answer and was ready to burst into the tent, when the pair emerged. Both were smiling.

"Everything is okay," Dr. Caffrey reported.

"What took you so long?" Burt asked. "You had all of us worried."

"Sorry," Ned replied. "We were talking about what might have happened to Nancy and me while we were unconscious."

Mr. Drew asked, "You have a new theory?"

Ned wondered if possibly some creature in the flying saucer communicated with the couple while they were asleep.

"How could he do that?" George asked.

Ned answered, "Perhaps he hypnotized us—told us what he wanted us to think, see, and do."

Bess shivered a little. "You mean someone controlled your mind?"

"I suppose it's possible," Ned replied.

"Even—even to make you believe you died and went to heaven?" Bess queried.

"Oh, sure," Ned answered with a chuckle.

By now Bess was absolutely terrified. "Do you realize that those weirdos may come back here and work on all of us?"

When Ned nodded, trying to tease her, she said, "Oh, don't say such things! You've scared me silly!"

Dave felt sorry for her. He sat down next to Bess and laid a comforting hand on her shoulder. "Don't be afraid. Ned is only kidding you."

"Oh, yes?" Ned asked.

Mr. Drew suggested they drop the subject in favor of preparing the evening meal. The newly arrived scientists went to their own quarters in the lab. The rest ate a delicious supper which Jan prepared. There was more conversation until about nine o'clock, when everyone started to yawn. Finally the campers went to bed.

It was a very warm night and Nancy, Bess, and George, who were together in one tent, decided to leave the side flaps halfway up. There was not a sound anywhere except the hoot of a distant owl.

Much later Nancy, sound asleep, thought a voice had called her name. She roused but did not open her eyes. Then she heard it distinctly.

"Nancy! Nancy!"

16

The Eerie Cave

Nancy managed to pull herself out of her deep sleep. She saw a figure standing over her. Instinctively she grabbed the flashlight from under her pillow and shone it into the mysterious face.

"Shoso!" she called.

Without a word he handed her a bunch of leaves, then turned and vanished. Nancy beamed her light on them.

The restorative leaves Bess had asked for! Great! she thought.

Hoping not to disturb her friends, the young sleuth got up quietly, took a plastic bag from her backpack, and put the leaves inside it. Finally she crawled back into her sleeping bag and dozed off.

The next thing she knew it was morning. The sun was shining through the trees, and birds were singing.

When the three groups of campers assembled to plan the day's work, Nancy showed the bag of leaves to everyone and told them about her night visitor.

Bess gaped at her friend in amazement. "And you didn't call George and me? Weren't you scared? Oh, I'd have died if I'd seen that man's stony face staring at me!" The others laughed.

Professor Hendricks, the botanist, asked for the leaves. "We'll analyze them this morning."

"They are unusual-looking," Dr. Caffrey said. "I don't recognize them."

"If you professionals don't recognize them," Mr. Drew remarked, "then I guess nobody would. Do you suppose this mountain forest is the only place in the world where the plant grows?"

"Maybe it's a tree," Bess suggested. "Let's find out from Shoso."

George had an idea. "We don't know where Shoso lives. Perhaps he has a garden and the leaves grow in it."

"Or," Jan said, and paused a moment, "maybe the tribe that once lived in this forest cultivated the plant, knowing its medicinal value."

"That's very possible," Dr. Caffrey agreed. "I'm

curious to see what you chemists come up with."

The botanist smiled. "I may even eat one of the leaves to sample its positive effect for myself!"

Since Nancy's group could do nothing to help, she suggested that the six young people continue their hunt for Old Joe's treasure.

"Where shall we start?" Dave asked, "and what shall we take?"

"I suggest you take hunting knives and that we begin at the pyramid of rocks I told you about," the girl detective answered. "We should see for ourselves where the arrow points."

The young sleuths put on waterproof hiking boots, packed a lunch, collected digging tools, and started off.

Hal called to them, "Bring us some fish!" He ran up to Dave and handed him a bucket with a punctured lid.

"Supper coming up," Dave replied with a grin. "A whole bucket full."

Nancy said, "Let's ride to the stream."

The group mounted. Nancy and George led the way to the marker inscribed with the initials of Old Joe's father. They tethered the horses and waded into the water.

The boys tried to catch trout with their hands. They thought it would be as easy for them as it was for Old Joe's dog, Trixie, but the slippery fish wriggled out of their grasp.

"There's a big one coming!" Dave shouted eagerly. "And I'm going to get it!"

He was about to grab the fish, when he slipped on a rock and fell, splashing water in every direction. The girls burst into laughter.

"Why don't you try it?" Dave said, disgruntled.

Ned and Burt were more successful. They put several fish into the bucket and fastened the lid. But as Ned dived for another speckled trout, he kicked over the bucket by accident. The lid came off and all of the fish they had caught swam downstream.

"We're pretty poor fishermen, I'd say," he chided himself.

Again the three girls giggled. "Maybe we're bad luck," Bess said. "Why don't Nancy, George, and I go on and let you boys catch fish by yourselves?"

The other girls agreed. They stopped to look at the pyramid. By pushing some stones aside they uncovered the initials and the arrow. It pointed directly across the bubbling stream.

When they reached the opposite bank, the searchers decided to separate. "Let's return in ten minutes to this same spot," Nancy suggested, "and report whatever clues we find."

The first time they met they were discouraged. "You don't suppose," Bess said, "that we're on a wild goose chase? Maybe Old Joe's father was a jokester."

"I think not," Nancy said. "I have an idea he was

serious, but wanted to keep his secret well hidden. Let's investigate beyond the immediate area this time."

Once more each girl went on her own, carefully examining every tree and rock. When the trio met again, George was grinning.

"I found something!" she exclaimed. "Follow me. Hurry!"

Bess suggested that they wait a few minutes for the boys. "We're already ahead of them. If we go too far, we could easily lose one another. I don't want us to get lost in this forest."

"Here they come now," Nancy said, glancing back on their trail.

The three boys were trudging up the short path the girls had made leading from the stream. Burt was carrying the bucket gingerly.

"Any luck?" George asked, then added teasingly, "Or did all those small speckled creatures slip away from you again?"

Burt smiled. "I'll show you."

He unfastened the lid partway. The girls gazed inside. To their amazement the bucket was full of trout!

"There's enough fish for everybody at camp," Bess remarked. "What a yummy supper. I can taste it now."

George led the group to a tree on which another

124

arrow had been carved. Underneath it, almost obliterated, were the initials *JA*.

"Joseph Austin!" Nancy exclaimed. "Super!"

"We're in luck!" Dave said.

The searchers set off in the direction indicated by the arrow. They trekked for some time, looking carefully at everything they passed, but there were no further directions. They kept on straight ahead, but became more discouraged by the minute.

Finally Nancy called a halt. "How about a rest period?" she suggested, dropping to the ground.

"Great idea," Bess replied. "And a good time to have that lunch we brought."

"Is that all you ever think about—lunch?" George replied.

"No," Bess smirked, "sometimes I think about dinner!"

Without waiting for another teasing remark from her cousin, Bess went to help with preparations. The snack was ready in minutes and eaten with gusto. Then the trekkers started off again.

"Wait a minute!" Nancy said. "I think we're going in the wrong direction."

"I agree," Ned told her.

They all returned to the luncheon spot, got their bearings, and started off once more. It was not long before they came to a good-sized tree with another carved arrow on it. They looked carefully for initials but if there had ever been any, they were gone now.

"Maybe Old Joe's father didn't put this arrow mark here," Burt suggested.

Nancy studied it closely. In her mind was a vivid picture of the other arrows.

"I'm sure this was made by the same person," she said. "I counted the number of little featherlike veins on the others. This one has the same amount."

Ned looked at her admiringly. "We didn't even see them, much less count them," he said. "Great sleuthing."

George noticed that this arrow pointed to a steep rise of land. When the climbers reached the top, they saw ahead of them a circular clump of trees that didn't seem part of the original forest, but looked as though they had been planted by someone. "Do you suppose that means something?" Dave asked.

Everyone rushed forward and then the boys squeezed behind the trees. A moment later, Ned called, "There's a cave here. It looks like a deep one."

He had scarcely finished speaking when they heard a nasty snarl and a hiss. The boys shrank back.

"Another wildcat!" Ned cried out, as the animal appeared at the cave entrance.

Nancy had a sudden hunch. "Maybe it's Kitty, Old Joe's friend. This may be her lair." She called out, "Kitty! Kitty! Where are you?"

The snarling and hissing ceased and the wildcat stopped short. Nancy continued to speak to her.

"Kitty, behave yourself! We're not going to hurt you!"

Finally Kitty came toward them. Did she recognize Nancy and Ned? Taking a chance, they patted the wildcat.

Bess was terrified. "You shouldn't do that!"

The animal looked up and for a moment they all panicked. Would she spring at one of them? But the big cat remained passive and quiet.

Nancy said to the others, "While Ned and I keep Kitty happy, why don't you four investigate the cave?"

"Will do," Dave replied.

The two couples walked behind the clump of trees and turned on their flashlights. In the meantime Kitty got a whiff of the fish in the bucket. She pawed at it, trying to push the lid off.

Nancy was afraid she might overturn the bucket and let the water run out. Then the fish would die. "Why don't we give Kitty one of the fish?" she suggested.

"Okay," Ned agreed. He selected a plump trout and threw it to the wildcat. She caught it in her mouth and ran off with the fish.

"I hope she doesn't return for more," Nancy said.

"Me, too," Ned added, with a grin.

Kitty did not come back, and everyone gave a sigh of relief. Ned hung the bucket on a high branch, hoping no other animal would try to disturb the fish. He and Nancy now entered the cave.

"Look what we found!" Bess exclaimed.

She and the others were examining pictures painted on the walls. They had dusted them off so the sketches could be seen plainly. One scene depicted a white hunter stalking toward an enormous tree. An Indian face was carved on the trunk.

George asked the others if they thought Old Joe's father had drawn the pictures, or whether an Indian may have painted them many years ago.

"It's very hard to say," Burt replied. "Whoever painted them was a real artist. The colors are perfect and haven't faded."

"They're great likenesses of Indians," Bess murmured, studying the paintings carefully.

In the meantime, Nancy was looking at another picture beyond the one of the big tree—a half-circle of footprints in front of a cave.

"I think this sketch refers to the cave we're in," she said, "and I think it's connected to the other picture of the hunter. The half-circle of footprints may lead from here to an enormous tree with an

Indian head on it. So let's get going! I have a hunch Old Joe's father really did draw these pictures."

"You mean we may be getting close to the treasure he buried?" Bess asked.

Yes, come on!"

17

Fire!

Undecided how to start hunting for the big tree with an Indian painted on it, Nancy's friends paced aimlessly. Which way should they go? There was no arrow to give them a clue.

Finally Ned broke the silence. "We're wasting time. I have a suggestion. After all, this is Nancy's mystery. Why don't we let her make the decision and we'll follow it?"

The others chorused their agreement.

Nancy smiled. "Thanks," she said. "The pictures indicate that we should half circle the cave until we reach an enormous tree with an Indian face on it."

"So," said George, "we ought to begin with small half-circles and keep making them larger until we find the right tree?"

Nancy nodded. The group spread out into parallel, semicircular formations and walked through the forest, examining every tree along the way.

"I think I found something!" Burt shouted excitedly. "Come here, everybody!"

His friends immediately ran toward him. Nancy was beaming as she darted past the others, hopeful that the search had ended successfully. When she reached him, Burt was on his hands and knees, brushing dirt away from the roots of a tree.

"Where's the Indian's face?" Nancy asked, as she glanced in puzzlement around the trunk.

"No Indian," Burt mumbled, still digging his nails into the soft ground. "Here!" he exclaimed at last.

Proudly he displayed the blunt tip of an arrow.

"Oh," Nancy said, secretly disappointed. "That's very nice."

"Nice!" Burt repeated. "Is that all you can say? It's *great!*"

By now, the others had gathered around the young man.

"So where's the Indian's face?" George inquired.

Nancy pointed to the arrowhead, and George said, "Is that all you found?"

Gradually losing his own enthusiasm, Burt nodded. To ease his regret, Nancy said, "I heard Jan say that Hal picked up a few old arrowheads not far from here. Maybe we ought to add this one to the collection."

Burt dropped the arrow in George's hand. "Be my guest," he said.

"Actually," George interrupted, "I'd like to wear it on a neck chain." She winked at Burt. "If you don't mind, that is."

"Of course I don't mind," he answered, evidently pleased.

The searchers continued their hunt for almost half an hour longer, but returned finally to their starting point. No one had discovered anything helpful.

Again Bess suggested they were on a wild goose chase, and once more the others disagreed with her. "Well, what do we do now?" she asked.

Nancy said that perhaps the half-circle of footprints in the cave picture might be the other half of the circles they had made.

"We'll retrace our steps, but instead of stopping halfway, we'll complete the circle."

George proposed that everyone change places. "Maybe someone else will spot what the others missed."

The group drew lots to determine who would take which circle. Nancy was assigned to the one farthest from the cave.

The search continued and no one spoke. Their

eyes were riveted to each tree they saw. Without discovering anything unusual they soon reached the end of the half-circle and went on to complete it fully.

Nancy had almost finished circling when she paused to gaze at a giant aspen tree. Apparently it had been struck by lightning. Half of it lay on the ground. The lower part of the trunk was still upright. There was no carving on this part.

The eager young detective hurried to the fallen trunk which lay bark side down. She could see part of a carving just above the break.

That looks like the carving of an Indian! Nancy thought, her pulse racing. She could not see it very well. If only she could roll the trunk over! But this was impossible. She called loudly to the rest of the group who flew to her side.

"Look!" she cried out, pointing. "Doesn't that look like the carving of an Indian's head?"

"It sure does," Ned agreed, adding with an obvious twinkle in his eyes, "Some people have all the luck. I knew I should have stuck with you!"

Nancy blushed happily. "I could've told you that," she teased back. "Come on and help me turn the trunk, everybody."

The six young people tried to push the fallen tree, but their efforts were in vain.

"This is aggravating," George fumed. "Especially

since I believe Nancy is about to solve the mystery!"

The young sleuth suggested that they examine the interior of the tree in case something was hidden inside. They combed every inch. The split was clean. There were no bumps or depressions.

"It would take a derrick to lift even half of this tree," Ned complained. "Nancy, what's our next move?"

"I think we should go to Old Joe's cabin and tell him what we've learned."

"This is maddening," Bess said in disgust. "I'm sure we're about to make a great discovery and can't do it because we're not strong enough."

Burt grinned. "Think of all the years this tree has lived here without being disturbed. It must be hundreds of years old. In fact, it might date back to the days of giant men who could lift it with one hand tied behind their back!"

Bess made a face at him, then turned to go with Nancy and the others along a trail they had made to where the horses were tethered. They mounted and, following the stream that Bess had almost tumbled into, headed for Old Joe's cabin.

Old Joe hobbled out to meet them. "Heard you all coming," he said. "You got some news for me?"

"Exciting news," Nancy told him.

The young people took turns telling the naturalist what they had discovered. At the end of their tale, his eyes opened wide in astonishment.

"You've done a magnificent job," he said. "I don't want to wait until my foot is entirely well before we move that tree. How about a couple of you going into town and phoning some lumberjacks to come up here and work on it?"

Ned volunteered. "I'd be glad to go. Tell me who to call."

Old Joe limped back into the cabin and wrote down the name and address of a tree-removal service that Ned would find listed in the telephone book.

"I'll start for town as soon as I get back to camp," Ned promised.

Old Joe told Ned about a shortcut he could take from the cabin to the village.

"Why not?" Ned replied.

Burt offered to go with him. Before the two set off, Nancy said, "Old Joe, how much should Ned tell the lumberjacks to do?"

The elderly man paused a moment. "First, he should let them turn the tree over so the Indian's head shows up. Then the men ought to leave so you young folks can look at it."

"Will do," Ned told him. He and Burt rode off.

Dave gave Old Joe one of the trout in the bucket, and Bess told him, "The boys caught the fish with their bare hands."

The naturalist laughed. "That's pretty clever. As clever as my Trixie, eh?"

Dave and the girls set off for camp. When they arrived, Nancy told only her father, Hal, and Jan what they had discovered.

"We have great hopes of locating the treasure," she explained, "but there's no use spreading the information until we're sure."

Ned and Burt reached camp just as supper was ready. The scent of frying fish whetted the appetites of the hungry campers.

Nancy revealed more of the day's adventure to the group. For a while everyone paid strict attention and asked many questions, but soon one, then another, began to yawn.

Finally Bess stood up. "I'm going to turn in," she announced. "Anybody coming?"

Before she could leave for her tent, some of the scientists joined the group. Nancy asked them if they had found anything new or unusual.

Dr. Halpern answered, "We've learned a couple of interesting things. None of the acid in Dismal Swamp has evaporated from the scorched area. It's very strong stuff."

Dr. York said that the chemists had worked on the chunks of sod that they dug up. We have come to the conclusion that the flying saucer sent out beams containing a combination of natural substances we know about and some secret ingredient. It is quite adhesive and difficult to separate for analysis."

His remark about a secret ingredient gave Nancy an idea. She asked, "Do you suppose the flying saucer came from some rival country and not from outer space?"

Dr. York smiled. "I would hate to think that another country is more scientifically advanced than we are!"

Dr. Caffrey also grinned. "Nancy, I thought you were convinced that you and Ned received thought waves from creatures in outer space. Wouldn't you hate to think that some rival country was able to control your mind?"

Nancy and Ned were horrified, and Ned said, "If men on earth did such a thing to us, I'm going to find them!"

"And do what?" Nancy prompted him.

Ned posed like a boxer. "Fight them, of course!"

Everyone laughed. Then the campers went to their tents and soon were sound asleep.

In the morning they awoke to the buzz of a giant motorized saw.

"Maybe the lumberjacks are cutting up the mystery tree!" Nancy exclaimed.

"How awful!" Bess said. "Why would they do that?"

"I don't know," Nancy replied. "Ned told them only to turn it over."

George jumped up. "But they could ruin the treasure!"

"Maybe even steal it!" Bess added, tears coming into her eyes.

Nancy thought the campers should get to the site at once. "Come on!" she urged. "Every minute counts."

The three boys joined the girls. All of them jumped on their horses and rode up the hill toward the fallen aspen tree.

George complained, "I think this oversized pony had lead feet." She urged him to walk faster.

Before the riders reached the spot, Nancy, in the lead, detected wisps of smoke curling up from the forest. "Look! Up ahead! Fire!" she cried out.

They could hear crackling and smell burning wood. Sparks were flying into the air and being blown about by the breeze; many of them fell to the ground. The fire, still some distance away, nevertheless was moving rapidly toward the valuable tree.

"Oh, this is dreadful!" Bess wailed. "Poor Old Joe! He mustn't be harmed."

Nancy's heart sank. Were Bess's words about to come true? Would a giant conflagration sweep through the forest, burn up Old Joe's treasure, his cabin—and possibly even injure him?

The fire might even destroy Dismal Swamp and the rare medicinal plants in the forest, the girl sleuth thought woefully.

Aloud she called in panic, "We must help put out the fire!"

18

A Rewarding Find

As the riders drew closer to the fire, they could hear men shouting. The young people wanted to urge their horses to go faster, but the climb was too steep. Nancy also feared that the animals might be frightened by the fire. Everyone reined in not far from the treasure tree.

"Fortunately the tree hasn't been harmed," Ned called to Nancy. He dismounted and hurried over to look. The lumberjacks had sawed the fallen trunk into sections and left them bark side down. The Indian's face was barely visible.

Nancy jumped from her horse and ran toward Ned. "Do you think we can turn the piece over?"

"Sure," Ned replied, watching a haze of smoke

141

drift through the surrounding trees. "But what about the fire?" If it gets too close, it could burn up Old Joe's treasure."

Nancy admitted that this had been her fear all along. "You're right and we must never let that happen. We must try to help the fire fighters at once. The blaze looks bad."

By this time the others had dismounted and were staring at the three girls' discovery. They all peered at what little they could see of the carving.

George said, "We'd better drag this section far away. It's too precious to lose. Hear the crackling of the fire?"

Indeed everyone could. How soon would it be before the flames spread in their direction?

Bess said, "Oh, I hope the fire doesn't get to Old Joe's cabin!"

Dave slipped an arm around Bess's shoulder. "A forest fire can really be frightening," he remarked. "When I was a little boy at camp, one started near us. We had to evacuate in the middle of the night without our daytime clothes. We were told to soak blankets in the nearby brook and put them over our heads as we went through the smoke."

Bess chided him, "Do you have to talk about such horrible things now? Isn't it bad enough that we're practically helpless?"

"Sorry," Dave said.

All the young people worked hard to stand the precious tree section on end. They zigzagged it as far from the fire as possible and laid it down carefully. For the first time the mysterious carving was turned faceup.

"That's gorgeous!" Bess cried out.

Nancy bent down for a close look at the carving. She exclaimed, "Here they are! The initials of Old Joe's father! I'm sure we've found the treasure."

She cut her exuberance short. "But we can't take time to study these clues now. We must help the lumberjacks fight the fire."

Burt suggested that the boys go back to camp for shovels to dig trenches as a backfire.

"And we'll bring axes to cut down underbrush," Dave added.

The smoke was thickening and the sound of burning wood grew frighteningly louder. The fire was spreading rapidly.

"I feel so helpless!" Nancy sputtered, coughing at the same time. "Let's move our horses down to where we dragged the big log. They should be safe there."

"Oh, I hope so," Bess wailed. "This is awful!"

As soon as that was done, the three girls hurried back up the hill. The fire was definitely closer.

"I'm afraid the fire is getting worse," George remarked.

143

"You're right," Bess added in alarm. "Oh, where are the boys?"

In a short time the three of them returned. They tethered their mounts with the other horses, then the girls helped them carry the shovels and axes to where they were going to start digging the backfire trenches.

"What can we do?" George asked immediately.

Ned suggested that they use the axes to chop down the underbrush and carry it away. "There may be enough dampness under the leaves on the ground to put out some of the flames."

"We'll try it," Nancy said.

While the girls worked diligently, the boys separated to spade up the ground in trenches some distance away from the fire. They lit matches and dropped them into the narrow furrows, igniting a blaze that snaked its way toward the already burning section.

"That should stop some of the spread," Burt declared, "but I think we should work faster."

The girls had already cut down and lugged away heaping piles of brush.

"That's great!" Ned called.

At the same moment they heard a helicopter overhead but could not see it through the dense smoke. No doubt the craft would be forced to stay above or behind the gray billows. In a few mo-

144

ments the group felt sprinkles of what they thought was rain.

Then Dave said, "There must be a forest ranger in that copter. He's pouring water on the blaze."

Bess sighed. "I hope it works!"

The young people continued to work hard even though they were exhausted and filthy. The girls were scratched from the thorny undergrowth they had been dragging away.

"I've never been hotter in my life," Bess said. "The fire must be getting closer."

Unfortunately her words were true. The roar of burning trees was louder than ever and more frightening. Would their work help quench the blaze?

As if in reply, the copter hovered directly overhead. Within seconds they were all drenched with water.

"Whee!" Bess exclaimed, running her hands through her soaked hair. "A free shampoo!"

The others laughed, then Ned remarked, "I guess the pilot missed his target."

"I'm happy he did," said George. "Now I feel cooler. I wish he'd come back and do it again!"

The pilot made no more misses, however, but continued to drench the smoldering trees.

After what seemed like hours of hard work, Nancy's group noticed that the fire was beginning to subside. The welcome deluge from the copter and the joint effort of the fire fighters had, at last, turned the conflagration into a soggy mess. Now they could see how large an area had burned.

"It didn't touch Old Joe's cabin," Nancy said with relief.

As she and her friends laid aside their tools and sank to the ground to rest, they saw two men coming toward them, threading their way among the charred stumps.

They introduced themselves as forest rangers. "We knew someone was helping from this end," one man said. "You young folks did a great job. We're mighty thankful to you."

"It was tough," Ned replied, "but I'm glad our efforts were useful."

As soon as the forest rangers were certain that the embers had died out, they left. Nancy turned eagerly to her friends. "Now we can continue our hunt for Old Joe's treasure."

They hurried back to the big log with the Indian's head carved on it. Nancy paused for several seconds before suggesting how to proceed.

"I think it would be safe to chip around the head and see if we can pry it up intact."

The three boys pulled out their hunting knives and carefully dug a circle around the carved picture. Finally they succeeded in removing it.

"Pretty neat," George remarked. "Nice souvenir

for hanging in your bedroom," she told Nancy.

The young sleuth smiled. "I'd love to have the carving, but I think it should go to Old Joe."

Nancy encouraged the boys to dig deeper. The chips flew as Ned, Burt, and Dave took turns with their strong, sharp knives. Suddenly they struck metal and stopped chipping.

"I think we found something," Ned told the others. Their pulses quickened at the thought that something exciting was about to happen.

Nancy watched closely as more of the wood covering the metal was chipped off. A box was revealed. There was writing on it. Nancy quickly dusted off the top.

On the lid these words were scratched:

For my son Joe Austin

"Old Joe's treasure!" the young sleuth exclaimed, hardly daring to believe her own words.

Ned attempted to lift the metal box from the depression in the tree trunk. No luck!

"Wait!" said Dave.

He and the other two boys burrowed down around the box with their knives until Ned could fix his fingers around it. To everyone's surprise the container was not heavy. Nancy wondered with a sinking feeling if it might be empty! Oh, it mustn't be, she thought.

The box was tightly sealed and there was no way to open it without special tools.

"Stymied again!" said Burt with a sigh.

"We shouldn't open it anyway," Nancy said. "Old Joe should. Let's go down to his cabin as fast as we can."

19

A Strange Reunion

When Nancy and her friends reached Old Joe's cabin, they found him lying on the bed. He complained of suffering a little setback with his foot and said it pained him to walk.

"It was my own fault," he said. "I thought I was stronger that I am. I tried to carry some logs in."

Suddenly he changed the subject. "I'm so glad all of you escaped the fire. Did it get close to your camp?"

Nancy assured him that the area had been miraculously spared and now the fire was entirely out.

Bess added, "The boys dug trenches for a backfire, and we girls cut down brush and dragged it away." She displayed several scratches on her forearms.

Old Joe glanced at the tiny cuts. "You ought to put some salve on those. Anyway, I'm glad nothing more serious happened to you. Personally speaking, I'm right proud of your group. I was really afraid my cabin might burn to the ground."

For the first time the naturalist noticed that Ned was carrying a rusty-looking metal box. Old Joe inquired, "What's that?"

"Nancy will explain," George told the elderly man, who sat up on the edge of his bed.

Ned placed the box alongside him. Old Joe stared at it unbelievingly.

"My name's on it!" he cried, excited. "Where did you find this?"

He cradled it in his hands affectionately as Nancy described their search in detail.

Old Joe shook his head. "To think I've searched this forest hundreds of times and never seen the pyramid of rocks or the cave with the Indian pictures in it!"

A look of fear glazed his eyes as he stared at the small box. "What if the forest fire had ruined everything forever?"

"But it didn't," Nancy said softly. "That's the important thing."

Old Joe nodded. "You're right. How can I ever thank you for saving that priceless log and the carving on it, not to mention what's inside? I'll always be grateful to you."

All this time Bess remained silent. It was clear, however, she was becoming impatient. "Why don't you open the box, Old Joe?"

The naturalist fingered the metal container lovingly. He smiled with tears in his eyes. "I'm almost afraid to open it," he mumbled quietly.

Ned told him that the boys would help lift the rusted lid. Did he have tools they could use? Old Joe pointed to a drawer where Ned found a chisel, a wedge, and a hammer. He used them to pry up the lid while Burt and Dave pushed as hard as they could with their fingers to spring the cover loose. Finally it gave way.

Old Joe peered inside. "Money!" he exclaimed in disbelief. "A lot of it! My father *did* outwit his enemy!"

Nancy was staring too. "And there are a lot of papers. They must be important messages from your father."

The elderly man's hand shook as he lifted out the first one. It was a long letter. He gave it to Nancy.

"Please read it for me. All of you have been so helpful to me the least—the least—"

He broke off, faintly whispering, and slumped back onto his pillow.

"Old Joe!" Nancy cried, letting the paper fall to the floor.

The other young people crowded around the

stricken man while Nancy felt his pulse. "It's very weak," she said. "Bess, please dampen that towel on the sink and bring it to me."

"Sure, Nancy."

George, in the meantime, stroked Old Joe's forehead. It felt cold and clammy.

"Please wake up," she murmured gently.

Within seconds Old Joe's eyes blinked open. A smile spread slowly across his face. "I'm all right," he said hoarsely. "Now help me sit up, will you?"

"Maybe you ought to lie there a little bit longer," Nancy said, patting his face with the wet cloth.

"But I feel fit as a fiddle." Old Joe grinned mischievously. "We'll compromise. You read the letter and I'll sit back. How's that?"

"Okay, if you insist," Nancy said. "But please promise to take a nap when I finish."

The man nodded. "Of course. After all, I don't have any plans to go wild boar hunting right this minute," he teased. "Now don't keep me in suspense any longer."

Without waiting another second, Nancy picked up the intriguing letter and read:

Dear Son:
This will come as a great surprise to you. At first you are not going to believe it, but I assure you it really happened to me.
Once I came up to the forest by myself.

That one time, an unearthly light suddenly appeared, approaching at tremendous speed from far off in the sky. I finally realized it was a flying object of some sort. To my amazement it slowed down and landed in Dismal Swamp. *It was a flying saucer!*

I rushed to take a close look at it—though the swamp smelled so bad it was overpowering. I heard a voice inside my head giving me orders. That was all I could hear—nothing out loud. The craft flew away almost as soon as it got here. I was terrified. At first I convinced myself that I must be dreaming. The silent voice warned me not to reveal the secret to anyone. Then the voice said the flying saucer would return to earth in ten years!

Old Joe exclaimed, "That's this year!"

The young people checked the date on the letter and confirmed it.

"Incredible!" Dave said.

"Go on, Nancy!" George begged.

The girl sleuth continued:

My son, you may wonder why I buried this information in a tree and carved an Indian's head on it. Now you will be

154

amazed to hear what else I have to say.

I never told you that your mother was a full-blooded Indian. She belonged to a small tribe of the Shawnee nation that used to live in this mountaintop forest. You had an older brother who looked just like her. He was mysteriously kidnapped, and I am sure he was taken away by the Indians, who did not approve of me.

Old Joe's eyes bulged. "An Indian brother! Shawnee!" he cried. "Now I'll never know who he was."

When exclamations of astonishment ended in murmurs, Nancy went on reading the letter.

Two years later you were born. Tragically, your mother died a few hours later. You showed no Indian traits. You look like me. I thought I never wanted you to find out about your mother and brother, but now I believe that in all fairness to you the truth should come out.

Old Joe interrupted to ask, "Does it say what my brother's name was?"

Nancy felt a lump in her throat. As she had been reading, a suspicion had entered her mind. She went on:

Your brother's name was Shoso.

"What!" Old Joe exclaimed. Everyone in the room except Nancy was stunned by the revelation.

Nancy said, "Come to think of it, Shoso and Old Joe do have the same build, and I noticed that their hands are almost identical. The main difference is in the color of their skin and Shoso's Indian face and hair."

Excitement ran high as everyone wondered if perchance Shoso knew the Austin family secret. Was this why he stayed in the forest?

"We must find him at once!" the naturalist announced.

Ned spoke to him calmly. "But how? We have no idea where he may be. We'll make a search, but he has never left a trail we could follow."

While Ned spoke, Nancy noticed another paper folded at the bottom of the box, and said, "More of the secret about your family may be revealed in this."

The elderly man leaned forward to pick it up and spread the paper on his lap. He looked at it for several seconds without speaking.

George, eagerly awaiting an answer, asked him, "What does the paper say?"

Old Joe explained that his father had written down a number of Shawnee Indian words. "Opposite them is the English translation," he said. He ran his finger down the list and exclaimed, "Here's the word for older brother! It's Ntheetha!"

He repeated the word several times as if trying to memorize it. "I hope I'm pronouncing it right," he said.

At this moment they all heard a noise outside the cabin. Slowly the door swung open. To their amazement Shoso was standing there!

At once Old Joe got up from the bed and hobbled across the floor, his arms outstretched in greeting.

"Shoso! Ntheetha!"

20

UFO Capture

A touching scene followed as Old Joe, forgetting his injured foot, hurried toward his newfound brother.

"Shoso!" he exclaimed happily.

The Indian in turn held out his hand, then pointed to himself, and said, "Ntheetha!"

None of the young people spoke as the men clasped each other around the shoulders and touched cheeks, first on one side, then on the other. Finally they backed apart, staring at each other in silence. Old Joe's face broke into a great smile and in response his blood brother grinned, too.

All this time Trixie stood quietly, her ears bent forward as she watched the reunion. Now, apparently feeling it was her turn to greet Shoso, the dog barked and jumped around. First she licked Old Joe's hands, then those of Shoso. Then she sat up between the two, waving her front paws.

The brothers patted the dog while Nancy and her friends laughed. Ned noticed a bone lying on a shelf. He picked it up.

"Okay to give this to Trixie?" he asked.

"Go ahead," Old Joe replied.

He went back to the bed and sat down with a sigh of relief. Nancy and George helped him ease back against his pillow.

"Are you feeling all right?" Nancy asked.

"Yes, yes," he insisted. "I guess the news kind of took my breath away for a minute."

Old Joe now picked up the sheet with the translated words. Using them, he spoke to Shoso. The Indian smiled at him and bobbed his head understandingly.

"Look how happy Shoso is," Bess whispered to her cousin. "Isn't it wonderful?"

"It's great," George said.

Nancy lowered her voice as she motioned to her group. "I think we should let these two brothers become better acquainted."

Everyone agreed. The young people said goodbye to the men.

On the way out Nancy stopped to speak to Old

Joe. "Please thank Shoso for bringing us those healing leaves. Ned and I and the scientists at camp are grateful to him. He may well be responsible for some wonderful new medical discovery."

The naturalist smiled. "It'll be hard to get your message across using the few words on this paper, but I promise to try," he said. "Good luck to you in solving the mystery of the flying saucer. Just remember—if I or Shoso can be of any help, let us know."

When the young people reached camp, Mr. Drew, Jan, Hal, and the scientists crowded around to hear the results of their search. All were amazed to learn not only of the treasure hunt but also the surprising story of the two brothers. "I must remember to call my friends the Dana Girls and tell them the outcome of all this," Nancy said, making a mental note.

"This is all absolutely fantastic," Jan remarked.

Hal added, "It certainly is. As a matter of fact, it's probably the greatest secret this old mountain has ever had!"

Professor Hendricks, the botanist, spoke up. "I'm not so sure that's true, however."

The scientist told his spellbound audience that Shawniegunk Mountain was filled with secrets. "We have men searching all over the place. This is a very special forest, indeed. It is a natural pharmacy filled with rare, unspoiled medicinal plants."

Nancy asked, "What is there besides the leaves Shoso gave us?"

Professor Hendricks replied, "The place is brimming with roots, plants, and leaves that are found sparsely in various parts of the world. Some are nerve medicines. The sap of one tree, if swallowed, is known to give instant relief for heart palpitations. We plan to take samples of these curative plants and herbs and grow them in quantity in other places."

Hal remarked, "It seems incredible that nobody has developed all this stuff."

This gave Nancy an idea. She said to Professor Hendricks, "I'm sure Shoso knows a lot about these plants. He might be a great help to you. Probably Old Joe will teach him to speak English and also keep him from disappearing all the time."

The botanist said he would appreciate the Indian's help. "I doubt, though, that he would ever want to leave this place. From what you've told me, I assume this is his ancestral home."

The day's happenings continued to be the topic of conversation throughout the evening meal. The group had just finished their supper when suddenly a glow of lights flashed brilliantly across the darkened sky. Then came a tremendous rush of wind that shook everything in sight.

"The flying saucer is coming back!" Nancy

gulped. "I don't believe it! Oh, how wonderful!"

Bess was fearful. She had experienced one similar windstorm and did not relish another. She cried out, "Be careful, everybody!"

The others in the camp paid no attention. They were too eager to watch the landing of the mystery ship. Everyone grabbed a flashlight or big camp lantern, and all made their way down the path to Dismal Swamp. They decided, however, not to use the horses and draw attention to themselves.

By the time the group reached the vicinity of the marsh, they saw the flying saucer overhead. It was vibrating convulsively and did not descend at once.

"The saucer must be in some trouble!" Nancy exclaimed.

As the campers watched, all the lights on the ship went out.

"Something is certainly wrong," Ned remarked. "Maybe it's antigravitational beams aren't working."

Within seconds the flying saucer dived for earth and crash-landed in the swamp. The next moment the craft turned on its side.

Dave said, "I hope it won't explode. Maybe we'd better get out of the way."

Everyone except Nancy and her father took his advice and ran into the woods a short way. The girl detective and her father did not move but watched the ship more curious than ever. It did not explode.

Bess, in the meantime, though still wary, edged back toward Nancy. "All we need is for it to catch on fire," she told the others. "Or rather, that's all we don't need."

Nothing happened to the spaceship and the campers descended once more to play their flashlights and lanterns on the mystery craft. It seemed as if the ship had died.

"Now what do we do, Nancy?" George asked.

Before the girl detective could reply, they heard another aircraft coming. Was it a backup flying saucer trying to help its sister ship out of trouble?

As the new craft appeared, the onlookers were puzzled. It was not the shape of the traditional round flying saucer, but was cylindrical, and on one side in large letters the word OPTIMUM was painted. The ship came down like a helicopter next to the disabled flying saucer.

"Wow! What a sight!" Ned exclaimed.

All the onlookers turned their flashlights on the ship. They saw the outline of a door. In a few seconds it opened and steps were lowered to the ground.

A man appeared in the doorway. He was wearing a uniform and the silver eagles of a United States Air Force colonel.

Mr. Drew stared at him, then exclaimed, "Colonel Aken!"

Nancy was dumbfounded. "You know him, Dad? The aircraft belongs to our country?"

"Yes, dear," her father answered, then walked forward to greet the colonel. As he came down the steps, several other airmen appeared. The campers moved ahead and everyone was introduced to the special group of Air Force men chosen to fly the *Optimum*.

Bess admired one young man who was blond and husky like Dave. "Isn't he cute?" she murmured in George's ear.

Dave pulled Bess by the hand toward Colonel Aken and Mr. Drew.

Nancy's father admitted he was surprised to see his friend in Dismal Swamp. "How did you happen to come here?" he asked.

Colonel Aken explained that when Mr. Drew had contacted the head of the Air Force and recounted Nancy's work on the flying saucer mystery, he was chosen to investigate.

"I also asked permission to try out this new American version of a flying saucer."

Nancy asked, "How did you know when the mystery ship was coming back?"

The colonel smiled. "I guess I have to let you all in on a secret—a government secret, actually. This wounded vehicle belongs to the U.S. It was built and launched ten years ago as an experiment, but disappeared shortly after. At the time not much was known about programming this particular type of spaceship. Of course, since then we've learned a great deal. The flying saucer suddenly reappeared at our experimental grounds but gave no clues as to where it had been, and so far as I know no sightings were ever reported."

When Colonel Aken paused, Nancy spoke. "I believe your flying saucer landed here in Dismal Swamp." She told him about the letter written by Old Joe's father.

The Air Force group was astounded. One of the young men, Major Tanner, remarked, "Mr. Austin must have been psychic to prophesy that our saucer would return to the same spot ten years later."

"Is this the identical ship?" Nancy asked.

"Yes," Colonel Aken replied. "It was worked on, reprogrammed, and sent out on a test flight. For a while it beamed back messages that all was going well. Then, as before, all communication ceased. We feared some rival country had captured our saucer."

Bess cried out, "That would have been a—a catastrophe!"

"I agree," the colonel replied.

"Where did you pick up the saucer?" Mr. Drew asked.

"About thirty thousand feet almost straight up. Our radar finally detected it. We felt sure the ship would return here, but its flight pattern was so erratic, it was hard to follow."

"I'd like to ask a question," George interrupted.

"I'll answer it if it's not classified," Colonel Aken replied, his eyes twinkling.

"Before the flying saucer arrived, the wind blew like a cyclone. Everything that wasn't tied down scattered."

"Yes," Bess added, "it actually blew away our picnic, even the fish cooking over an outdoor fire."

The Air Force men laughed. Colonel Aken said, "Young lady, you did hit upon classified information. Yes, the flying saucer caused the windstorm. Sometimes rain follows. How and why, I'm obliged to tell you, must remain a government secret. Sorry to disappoint you."

"But your new ship, the *Optimum*, didn't cause a windstorm," Nancy remarked.

Colonel Aken looked at her searchingly. "You have a very keen mind. It's true. This newer ship was built from totally different plans and will accomplish more than the earlier model. Again, however, I am not at liberty to give you additional information."

Ned admitted he was puzzled about why the old flying saucer whirled as it flew.

The colonel said with a knowing grin, "After you graduate from college, enroll in our technical training school. We'll be happy to teach you some of our trade secrets."

Suddenly Nancy realized the mystery had been completed. The girl detective felt sad to think her work was over. In a short time, however, she would become involved in solving the mystery of *The Secret in the Old Lace*.

She snapped out of her reverie and asked the officer, "Will the old saucer ever be able to fly again?"

"We'll try to find out very soon," Colonel Aken answered, "but first, in honor of your helping us find her, I think we should reward you with a little trip in our *identified* flying object." He smiled. "Tomorrow all of you will have a chance to ride in the *Optimum*. You'll be the first civilians to do so."

Nancy and her friends as well as the scientists were thrilled by the prospect and applauded Colonel Aken for his invitation.

He in turn held up his hand for silence. "Don't give me any credit for recovering the mystery ship. I believe it all belongs to Nancy Drew, her father, and her friends. What do the rest of you say?"

Professor Hendricks called out, "We say yes!"

A great cheer rang through the forest.

Don't Miss

THE HARDY BOYS ® MYSTERY STORIES
by Franklin W. Dixon

Night of the Werewolf #59

Mystery of the Samurai Sword #60

The Pentagon Spy #61

The Apeman's Secret #62

The Mummy Case #63

Mystery of Smugglers Cove #64

The Stone Idol #65

The Vanishing Thieves #66

NANCY DREW MYSTERY STORIES ®
by Carolyn Keene

The Triple Hoax #57

The Flying Saucer Mystery #58

The Secret in the Old Lace #59

The Greek Symbol Mystery #60

Plus exciting survival stories in
The Hardy Boys ® Handbook
Seven Stories of Survival
by Franklin W. Dixon with Sheila Link